SPENCER COHEN, BOOK THREE

THE SPENCER COHEN SERIES

N.R. WALKER

COPYRIGHT

Cover Artist: Reese Dante
Editor: Boho Edits
Spencer Cohen Series © 2016 N.R. Walker
Publisher: BlueHeart Press
Second Edition: 2023

ALL RIGHTS RESERVED:

WARNING

Intended for an 18+ audience only. This book contains material that maybe offensive to some and is intended for a mature, adult audience. It contains graphic language, explicit sexual content, and adult situations.
The author uses Australian English spelling and grammar.

TRIGGER WARNINGS:

Suicide. Reader discretion advised.

TRADEMARKS:

DEDICATION

This series is dedicated to every Spencer out there: for those who have lost everything but still have hope, for those too afraid to love again but crave it all the same, for those who have been through hell yet are still strong enough to smile, and for those who wear their scars inked into their skin.

THE SPENCER COHEN

SERIES BOOK THREE

N.R. WALKER

ONE

On Saturday morning, I was manning the reception counter in the tattoo shop while Emilio was finishing up inking some guy. I flipped through the latest tattoo magazine, humming happily to myself, when the reason for my happy humming walked through the door.

Andrew.

God, I could just drink him in. I was so smitten with seeing him, I didn't really even notice the two people who came in with him.

"Hey," he said, giving me a quick kiss. He looked just as happy to see me and kept his hand on my back. "Spencer, this is Shell."

Oh, yes. He worked with Shell, which was short for Michelle. They both did visual animation at DreamWorks. I'd given Andrew tattoo magazines to give to her and had spoken to her on the phone once during the week, very briefly. "Nice to finally meet you."

"Likewise. I've heard all about you," she said with a smile, and Andrew rolled his eyes. Shell introduced me to the woman beside her. "This is my girlfriend, Wendy."

I shook her hand. "Spencer Cohen."

Michelle looked me up and down but soon grinned. "I can see why Andrew gets that glazed-over look when he talks about you."

He pushed her arm. "Shut up."

Shell just laughed. "It's true. I work with him every day, and he never shuts up about you."

He groaned and glared at them. "Anyway, Shell was the one who I borrowed the tattoo magazines for, and I told her to come in to see Emilio. Just to see about placement and stuff, not an actual tattoo."

"Not yet, anyway," Shell said. "But soon."

"He'll be free in about half an hour," I told them. "Wanna take a seat?"

We sat in the little waiting area we often frequented for morning coffees and late night dinners, and Andrew sat right beside me and quickly held my hand.

"So what have you got in mind?" I asked Shell.

"Oh, I've drawn it already," she said. "Well, the general idea. Andrew helped with body movement and that kind of thing."

I looked at Andrew. "You did, huh?"

He shrugged and smiled smugly. "Like I said before, it's what I do. Just Emilio's canvases move. Mine don't."

Shell had taken out a piece of paper from her bag and handed it to me. On it was a perfect interpretation of Peter Pan. "Wow."

"It's pretty cool, huh?" she asked. "He's always been my favourite character."

Then out came another piece of paper. "And this one I drew for Wendy. We were gonna get them done together." Shell smiled at Wendy.

The second drawing was of course Wendy from Peter Pan and Tinkerbell. I looked at both girls. "They're really great."

Emilio soon finished and joined us, inspecting the drawn pictures. "You really drew these?"

Shell nodded. "Yep."

Then suddenly I had a great idea. I looked at Andrew and squeezed his hand. "You should draw something for me."

Andrew blinked. "A tattoo?"

"Yeah," Emilio said, nodding enthusiastically. "Totally. Then the girls can see how it works."

"Yes," I agreed. "I've been talking about getting another one." I held out my arms, which were covered. "I just didn't know what or where to put it."

Emilio handed Andrew a piece of paper and a drawing pen. Andrew blanched. "Right now? For Spencer to get tattooed *right now*?"

I nodded. "I'm up for it."

"Yes!" Shell cried. "You should!"

Andrew put the pen to the paper and stopped and stared at me. "Will you seriously get whatever I draw tattooed on your body?"

"Absolutely."

He lay the pen on the paper. "Then I will wait and work on it properly. I want it to be perfect."

"Okay, for a bigger piece that's fair enough," I said. "So draw me something super quick and small. I have a spot here," I showed him near my elbow, the blank space about the size of a quarter.

"You're still going to get it tattooed, though?" Andrew asked.

"Well yeah, but it's tiny, and it will blend into the sleeve as a whole. Just something quick and small."

He shook his head as he tried to think of something. "Um..."

Then Emilio said, "When you think of Spencer, what is the first thing that comes into your mind?"

Andrew looked at me for a long second, then he smiled. Putting pen to paper, it took him half a second to draw. Only it wasn't really drawn, it was written. He turned it around to show me. I stared at it, and he quickly explained, "It's a treble clef and 6/8 time."

I looked up at him then. I knew exactly what it meant.

"It's for the song 'Hallelujah'," he went on to explain to the others who were watching us. "The sheet music starts with that."

I couldn't take my eyes off him. I didn't know what to say. It was so perfect, and he looked at me and smiled. "You like it?" he asked.

I shook my head, no. "I love it. It's um..."

Emilio, oblivious to the moment Andrew and I were having, took the piece of paper. "Cool." He tapped my leg. "Come on, I'll do it now."

Still not taking my eyes off Andrew, I stood up and went to follow Emilio. Except I only got a few steps and went back to where Andrew was still seated, lifted his face, and kissed him. "It's perfect."

I left him breathless and blushing and planted myself on Emilio's chair. He had inked me many times so it was a familiar, almost cathartic experience. While Emilio got his gear ready, I sat back and got comfy. Andrew walked over cautiously. "Can I watch?"

"Of course," I said, holding out my free hand.

He quickly took it. "I can't believe you're just going to get something I drew tattooed on your skin."

"I love it."

"But it's really permanent."

I laughed. "Yes, tattoos are. That's quite correct."

"Shut up. You know what I mean."

"I do."

"What if you change your mind?"

"I will never not love that song," I told him. "And the fact you knew to draw it for me, that makes it more special."

"Girls?" Emilio called out. "Want to come watch?"

Shell and Wendy came over and Emilio explained the equipment and the process. He positioned my arm accordingly, and in the small space of uninked skin, he tattooed the music notation.

Andrew squinted at me, as though he could feel the pain. "Does it hurt?"

I shook my head. "Nah." He didn't look convinced, so I held up the arm that was joined to the hand he was still holding. "If it hurt that much, would I be covered in them?"

He shrugged, not looking at all convinced, but he leaned over me to take a closer look. I didn't mind because he could lean over me any time he liked. He was warm and smelled so damn good, but then he let go of my hand and walked around to Emilio's side to get a better view. He was studying his handiwork. "Great lines."

"Thanks, man," Emilio said, not breaking concentration. It literally took him all of two minutes. He sat back to inspect his work and wiped the area one last time. "Done."

I jumped up and walked over to the mirror, inspecting my new addition at different angles. "Looks good."

When I turned back, Andrew was biting his bottom lip, all kinds of nervous. "You like it?"

I walked over to him, and putting my hand on his waist, I kissed his cheek. "Love it." I sat down again, and Emilio showed and told Shell and Wendy about aftercare and how best to look after any tattoo they might get. I let him wrap the small area, and when he was finishing up, I asked them, "So? Ready to book your first appointment?"

They both nodded excitedly. "Yeah, for sure," Shell said.

"Right, then," I said, leaving Emilio to clean up his station. I led the two ladies over to the reception counter. "What day?"

They decided on the next Saturday. I booked them both in and took copies of their artwork for Emilio to keep safe. They were buzzing with excitement and decided to spend the afternoon at Venice Beach. "Andrew? Wanna come with us?"

He gave me a quick glance and shook his head. "No, but thanks anyway."

Shell laughed knowingly, and Andrew told her to shut up, but he blushed, and that only made her laugh some more. I put my arm around him and pulled him into my side. "He has a much better offer."

"I bet he does," Shell said, and with a smiling kiss to his cheek and promises to see him at work, they walked out the door.

Andrew breathed in deeply before pulling away. "Does your arm hurt?"

Well, there were one of two ways I could play this. One, tell him the truth that no, it certainly did not hurt. Or two, play it for everything it was worth. "It's a little tender," I said, making a face and favouring my arm.

He pulled back, concern etched on his face, and took gentle hold of my freshly tattooed arm. "Really?"

"Yeah, I might need to lie down," I said pretending to be serious. "And you might need to join me."

Emilio snorted as he finished disinfecting the chair I sat in, which made Andrew look sharply at me. "You're joking, aren't you?"

"No," I said, trying not to smile. "I need lots of attention of the fornication variety."

Andrew dug his fingers in my ribs, making me jump. "In that case, you can buy me lunch."

"Good because I'm starving."

"And we need to go back to the music shop," he said. "Because as good as the Jeff Buckley album is, there's only so many times you can listen to it."

I gasped, faking offence. "You wound me. There *is* only so many times you can listen to it, and that number is infinity."

"Infinity is not a number."

"Yes it is." I walked to the door and opened it, waiting for him to walk out first. "After you."

"You have to pick me a new album to listen to this week," Andrew said, then he stopped and turned back to Emilio. "Oh, Emilio? Want us to grab you anything to eat?"

Emilio glanced quickly at me, then smiled and nodded slowly. "Yeah, that'd be great. Thanks."

I put my arm around Andrew's shoulders and dragged him out the door. "Don't try sucking up to my friends. Emilio will always agree with me. Infinity *is* a number."

We could hear Emilio chuckling as the door closed behind us, and I smiled all the way up to the burger joint, with Andrew under my arm and a little piece of him freshly inked into my skin.

TWO

Andrew finished his burger and sat back in his seat, happily patting his belly. "So, what did you do this morning?" he asked.

I pushed my half-full plate away, baffled at how much he could eat. "Woke up alone." I sniffed. "Where do you put all that food?"

"I burn it off at the gym. Would also explain why you woke up alone. I told you I was leaving."

"I can think of plenty of other ways to burn calories."

He blushed, but his smirk gave his interest away. "Is that so?"

"Yep. And you don't even have to wear gym clothes."

"Would I be wearing *any* clothes?"

"Absolutely not."

He laughed. "Didn't think so."

"Truthfully, the fact you hide that body with any kind of fabric is a crime against humanity."

He almost spat his drink, but he composed himself. "I'm not sure all of humanity would agree."

"Then they're either wrong or liars. Or lesbians. Or in the anti-argyle society."

He burst out laughing. "Anti-argyle society?" He looked down at his argyle-patterned vest. "If they were anti-argyle, then wouldn't that mean they don't like me wearing it? Therefore they'd side with those who prefer me to not wear clothes, not those that do?"

"Don't correct me with logic and reasoning and intelligence. It was funnier the way I said it."

He laughed again and looked at me with soft, warm eyes. "So? Ready for your hot date tonight?"

My great mood just took a nosedive into Crapville. "It's not a date."

"I was joking."

I frowned at my drink. We'd been through this before. "It's work. I'm being paid to be there. If it were my choice, I'd be spending the night with you. You have to know it's just a job to me."

He put his hand up. "Spencer, I was just kidding."

"Sorry." I sighed. He said he was kidding, but I had to wonder... "Andrew, please tell me you're okay with it?"

"I am." He reached over and took my hand. "I am. I know it's just a job. I was just joking. It was supposed to be funny because I know going to some formal dinner with a stuffy, old guy is the last thing you'd actually want to do."

"Stuffy, old guy?"

"Well, that's what you called him."

"True."

"And I should be able to joke about it," he said. "Because tonight, while you're sitting in a corporate dinner with a man you don't like, listening to speeches from people you don't know from a company you don't work for, I'll be curled up on your papasan chair reading a book and listening to the new album you're about to buy me."

I found myself smiling at him. "Still not funny."

He chuckled. "Yes it is. I might even go down and hang out with Emilio until he closes up shop."

My mouth fell open. "I hate you."

He grinned. "No you don't. And don't leave your mouth open like that or I might be tempted to put something in it."

Now I laughed. "We could go into the bathroom?"

He rolled his eyes and picked up a french fry from my plate. He wielded it like a weapon. "I'd be tempted to put one of *these* in your mouth, Spencer. One of these."

"I like my idea much better."

He shoved the french fry into his mouth and climbed out of the booth. "Come on then."

I looked up at him all excited. "Really?"

"No, not in some diner bathroom," he whispered, collecting Emilio's burger-to-go off the table. "Music store, then your place. *Then* you can do what you like with me."

"Promise?"

"Depends on the album you buy me."

"Is that blackmail?"

"Nope. Think of it more as a pay and reward scheme."

I rolled my eyes and walked to the door, which I dutifully held open for him. "Just so you know, I'm not opposed to blackmail. If it means I have you in bed for the rest of the day I'm all for it."

He laughed and held out his hand. "May I hold your hand?"

"You may," I said, but then pulled my hand away at the last second. "Depends on whether I have full discretion on the album I choose for you."

He narrowed his eyes at me as he considered my counter. "Hmm, you drive a hard bargain. But fine."

I held out my hand, and he grabbed it quickly, probably before I could add any more terms and conditions. I was grinning as we walked up the street hand-in-hand.

"And just so you know, if the music is crap, I might have to call veto on the condition of being in your bed all day."

I barked out a laugh. "Just as well I have impeccable taste. And," I added, "I'm not opposed to having you on the sofa instead."

He chuckled. "I still haven't figured out how we could use that papasan chair."

I stopped at the music store, but before I opened the door, I leaned in and whispered, "If I choose the best album for you today, I shall fuck you in that chair when we get home."

He blushed and his pupils blew out, his voice was breathy. "And how will you know if it's the best album?"

"Believe me, I'll know." I opened the door and waited for him to walk inside. Andrew went straight to the jazz section, but I headed straight for the counter. I waited for the clerk to finish doing whatever it was he was doing. "Hi. I ordered in a record. Wilhelm Kempff's *Moonlight Sonata*."

The cashier clicked his fingers. "Yes! Came in yesterday. Not every day we get requests for classical. I'll just grab it from out of the storeroom."

Andrew walked quietly up behind me. "Spencer? What did you do?"

I smiled at him. "I might have pre-ordered you something."

"You cheated?"

"I didn't cheat. I just changed the way the game is played."

He shook his head. "Do I want to know what it is?"

The cashier came back to the counter, record in hand.

"Here it is. Not easy to get. The DGG vinyls aren't too common these days, even second-hand." He handed it to me, and taking the wrapped up burger from Andrew, I gave the record straight to him.

He stared at it and swallowed hard. "It's Kempff's 1965 performance with the Berlin Philharmonic in Berlin..." He shook his head, still looking at the record cover. "Spencer..."

"Did I do perfect?"

Then he looked up at me. His eyes sparked with something I wasn't sure I'd seen before. "You did."

The cashier took the album and checked it for scratches before he re-sleeved it. I paid some indecent amount of money for it, thanked the cashier, and we left. Only we didn't get too far. Andrew stopped just a few steps up the street. "I can't believe you did that," he said, still holding the album like it was the holiest of grails.

"It wasn't that hard," I explained. "You said *Moonlight Sonata* was your most favourite song. So, of course I googled best performances and read some forums to see what classically like-minded people thought, and this guy—" I pointed to the old dude on the cover "—came up time and time again."

"No." Andrew shook his head like I missed the point. "That you would do that for me. That you would put that much thought into something to make me happy."

"Does it?" I asked. "Make you happy?"

"Incredibly."

"I ordered it a few days ago," I told him. "I kinda forgot about it until you mentioned getting a new album. I didn't even know if it had come in yet."

"And you made a bet for the most perfect album without knowing you could get it?"

"Sure. I just would have found you something else."

He slowly shook his head. "Not as perfect as this."

"Now that you mention that bet," I said thoughtfully, "may I suggest we go back to my place and christen the papasan chair?"

He chuckled, and a faint blush crept over his cheeks and down his neck. "You were never going to lose that bet."

I put my arm around his shoulder, and we started to walk again. "Never. Unless there's a B Side somewhere of Jeff Buckley playing Beethoven, I don't think the most perfect album actually exists."

We dropped off Emilio's lunch, and when we got back to my flat, I took the album from Andrew and slid it onto the dining table. I wasted no time in kissing him. I cradled his face with my hands and led him backwards to the papasan chair. Granted, circular, dish-shaped chairs that moved weren't exactly suitable for sex, but this was a challenge I wanted to accept. And conquer.

He'd been eyeing off this chair for the weeks he'd been coming here, and he'd even mentioned a few times that he'd wondered how suitable it was for sex. So I knew he wanted to try this.

He pulled his mouth from mine. "Bathroom," he whispered, then disappeared through the bathroom door.

I missed the taste of his mouth already. But figuring he was going to be a few minutes while he cleaned himself up a bit, I collected some supplies from my bedroom, leaving the lube and condom on the papasan chair. Then I put the record on the turntable but didn't play it. Not yet.

When he came back out, he wore nothing but a towel around his waist and a nervous smile. God, he was so gorgeous. I moaned at the sight of him, the promise of what his being naked meant. My cock pulsed in anticipation.

Andrew slowly walked over to the papasan chair and bit his bottom lip. "Um."

"Kneel on it," I murmured. "Hold the top edge like handlebars."

While he did that, I undressed, tossing my clothes somewhere behind me. I was too busy watching Andrew to notice anything else. He'd lain the towel over the padded papasan cushion and knelt, thighs spread wide and his arms stretched to grip the top edge of the chair. He looked perfect.

Still standing on the floor, I reached between his legs and rubbed his balls and gave his cock a few strokes until he let his head fall forward and he moaned. Then I smeared lube over my fingers and found his hole, rubbing across his entrance, then slipping a fingertip inside him.

By the time I'd added a second finger he was rolling his hips and making the most delicious sounds. He threw his head back, and his tone had the bite of impatience. "Spencer."

Taking that as my cue, I stepped back and gently lowered the tonearm of the record player. The familiar crackle of a vinyl recording filled the room as I rolled on the condom and applied more lube, then knelt behind him. I leaned in and spoke gruffly into the back of his neck. "Ever been fucked to your favourite song?"

Goosebumps broke out over his skin, and he let out a nervous breath, half laugh, half need. "No."

I pressed the head of my cock against his ready arse as the melodic piano music started, teasing him as the music teased the air. When the intro morphed into something more, I pushed into him.

Andrew groaned as I filled him. His head fell forward as he gripped the top of the chair, and the muscles in his shoulders flexed tight, distracting me from the pleasure building, from how good he felt.

The chair started to tip, with the weight of both of us at one end. So I leaned down, pushing Andrew forward a little and pushing into him fully at the same time. He cried out, a mix of pain and pleasure I knew well. I leaned over him and kissed his shoulder, his neck, and whispered in his ear, "You're so fucking hot."

He arched his back, pushing his head back and giving me more of his arse. "Spencer," he murmured. The music took off in the second movement, complex and amazing, and I thrust into him in 3/4 time.

Andrew reached back blindly and found the back of my head, keeping my lips at his ear. He was arched like a bow, impaled on every inch of me, and we kept perfect rhythm with Beethoven.

I reached around his body and gripped his cock. He was hard, and the precum at his tip made my hand slick as I stroked him. But I was too far gone to wait for him. He felt too damn good, and I was already so on edge.

"Spencer," he grated out. "Fuck."

And that was all it took. My name from his lips and a whispered curse and the coil in my balls sprang, surged, and my orgasm roared through me like wildfire. I gripped his hips and thrust into him one final time as I filled the condom. The room spun, silent and loud at the same time, and I almost lost balance.

Before I had fully come to my senses, Andrew was now standing in front of me. I was somehow on my feet and he had his hands on my arms to steady me. "You okay?" he asked with a laugh.

"Mmm."

He grabbed my hand and led me to my bedroom, where

he all but pushed me onto my bed face first. "Lie down. We're not done."

I laughed, muffled, into my pillow. "I tried to hold back, but that was too fucking hot."

Not aware of much else around me, I felt the bed dip before he pushed my thighs wider apart. Then there was cool liquid and fingers probing me, without warning, without apology. I groaned and gripped the bedcovers, suddenly more coherent. I loved being manhandled in bed. And I loved that Andrew, quiet, shy and geeky Andrew, was the complete opposite of that when it came to sex. He was in charge. There was no doubt. I lifted my arse for him. "Yeah. Like that," I urged him.

He added more fingers and fucked me for a minute. One hand pushed down on my back, one hand at my entrance, he was leaning over me. I knew his huge cock was next, and I wanted it. I needed it. "Andrew."

He pulled his fingers out of me, and while he applied the condom, I put pillows under my hips and laid back down for him with my face in the mattress and my arse in the air. He wasted no time. He simply positioned himself behind me, put his cock to my hole, and pushed into me.

He wasn't gentle. He wasn't slow. He leaned forward and breached me, stretched and filled me. I groaned loudly, gritting my teeth. "Fuck. Your cock is huge."

He stilled, his breath hot on my back. "You okay?"

"Fuck yes," I told him. "Jesus."

He gave me a second to adjust and then slowly started to rock into me. His voice was a gruff whisper. "You didn't make me come before."

I laughed into the mattress. "Remind me to fail next time, too, if it means you'll fuck me like this."

He thrust harder, making me cry out. Then he did it again

and again until he stilled. His fingers dug into my hips, and he pulsed inside me. Jesus, I could feel him come. His voice was a strangled cry as he pulled out and collapsed on top of me; his chest was heaving, and his breaths were ragged.

I couldn't move. I was pinned underneath him. His body was a glorious weight, and when he rolled off me, I felt the absence immediately. I shuffled around so I faced him and kissed him. "Wow."

"I've never done that before," he whispered, his eyes closed. It was as though he couldn't bear to look at me.

"Never done what before?" I asked. "Fucked some guy into the mattress?" He nodded, still not meeting my eyes. "Andrew, seriously, you can do that to me every day of the week."

He looked at me then. "Are you sore?"

I wrapped my arm around him and pulled him against me. "That was incredible. No, I'm not sore." I wiggled my arse. "Well, maybe a little, but that's because you're hung like a horse."

His reaction was a mix of amused and horrified. "Oh my God. Did I hurt you?"

I laughed. "No. Like I said, you can have me like that any time you want."

"Oh." Andrew chuckled, still obviously embarrassed. "I don't know what came over me."

"I know what came over you. Because I got you close to orgasm on the papasan chair, but I came first because, well, you were so fucking hot, and apparently *close to orgasm* wasn't good enough for you."

He barked out a laugh, flushed a full shade of red, and ducked his head into my chest. "God, Spencer. You can't just say stuff like that."

I drew in a deep breath and sighed. "You are a

confounding man, Andrew Landon. Tiger in bed, kitten out of it."

He pulled his head back quickly and stared at me. "What?"

He made me laugh. "You have no idea, do you?" I took his blank stare as my answer. "It's what I find so enthralling about you. You look like a shy, mild-mannered guy, but underneath you're really just a bossy top."

His eyes almost popped out of his head. "A bossy top?" He scoffed. "I don't think so."

"Oh, I'm sorry, were you not here ten minutes ago? Because I'm pretty sure you just bossy-topped me into the mattress."

He made a whining sound and shook his head. I think he was genuinely horrified. "I'm not... I don't... I'm not just a top."

"No, you're a bossy bottom too."

"I'm not bossy," he said quietly. "Well, I don't mean to be."

I held his face and kissed him. "You're perfect. Don't change a thing."

He gave me a small frown. "I'm not perfect. You keep saying I am, but I'm not."

I rolled us over until I was on top of him. I put both hands to his face and kissed him again, deeper this time. When I pulled away, I waited for him to open his eyes and look at me. "You know what would make you absolutely perfect?"

"What's that?"

"It's a pretty big ask, but I'm sure you'll manage absolutely-perfect status." I rolled off him, got off the bed, and walked to the door. "Pick a movie and make some popcorn."

"And that will make me perfect?"

"Yep. I'm going to have a shower."

He called out, "And you think I'm bossy?"

"Yes, I do." I went into my bathroom and my smile grew even wider when I saw his toothbrush next to mine in the holder. It was crazy how happy something so simple made me. Not that I'd ever admit to Andrew how seeing his toothbrush next to mine made my heart thump funny because I'm certain he'd think me mad. Or a romantic sap. Or both.

My smile cut short when he followed me into the shower —literally into the shower cubicle and the streaming water. He was still naked, but I could tell something was wrong by the look on his face. "Andrew?"

It was like something couldn't wait, as though he had to tell me what was on his mind in that second or he'd die. His brow furrowed. "I know I'm bossy but I don't mean to be. You make me forget to censor myself."

Standing under the stream of water, I opened my mouth to speak, but he wasn't done.

"With Eli, I had to watch what I said or did because I didn't want to scare him off. I never spoke my mind. I never took charge and ordered him around in the bedroom like I just did with you." He swallowed hard and blinked at the spray of water on his face. "But I can be me around you. I *am* bossy. I like things done a certain way. I'm a perfectionist, but I'm *not* perfect. You see the real me. This is who I am."

To say I was stunned at his outburst was an understatement. Stunned, floored, amazed. And speechless. I pulled him to me then pushed him against the tiles and kissed him with as much honesty as he'd shown me. No, I couldn't find the words in that moment, but I hoped he understood me anyway.

When I finally pulled away, both of us breathless, I kept my lips to his. "Don't ever censor yourself," I whispered. "Don't change a thing." I stared into his eyes, and amid the steam and ragged breaths, his gaze never left mine. "You are perfect."

He shook his head. "No, I'm not."

"For me. You're perfect for me."

He finally smiled, and lifting his hand to my chin, he scratched my beard. "Don't be long. I'll put the popcorn in the microwave."

He walked out of the shower, drying himself quickly, and putting on nothing more than the towel around his waist as he disappeared out of the bathroom. I smiled to myself as I washed my body and shampooed my hair, and then I remembered... Popcorn. Microwave.

Shit!

The only popcorn I had wasn't supposed to go in the microwave. It was some organic, gourmet stuff that had to be cooked on the stove. *Shit, shit, shit!* I shut the water off, and grabbing a towel, I scrambled out of the bathroom and ran into the kitchen while trying to wrap the towel around my hips with my hair full of shampoo. "Andrew!"

He was standing there, still with just a towel around him, holding the whole bag of popcorn with the microwave door open. I startled him. "What?"

"Not the microwave," I panted. I closed the microwave door and put my hand to my heart. "Popcorn goes on the stove. In a pot. With oil. And maybe not the entire bag, unless we want to feed the masses."

He looked at the bag like it had offended him. "I didn't think it looked like the ones my mom used to make."

I barked out a laugh. "Didn't want to read the instructions on the packet?"

"Well, no, I just thought..." The corner of his mouth pulled down. "I told you I don't cook. You give me the 'you're so perfect' speech, and I try to kill us with popcorn."

I took the popcorn from him and gave him a quick peck on the lips. "You're still perfect." But then shampoo ran into my eye. I squinted my eyes shut. "Ow, shit, shit. My eye!"

Now he laughed and, taking my arm, led me back to the bathroom. "Keep your eyes shut," he said. I heard the water turn on and felt him pull my towel away before he took my hand and gently pushed me into the shower.

I stuck my head straight under and let the water stream over my face and eyes while washing the shampoo out of my hair. It only took a minute, and when I was done and dried, I threw on a pair of cargos and found Andrew dressed, sitting on the sofa with his bare feet on my coffee table. He had two bottles of water and a bowl of crisps. "I got them from your cupboard. Figured they were safer than popcorn."

I lifted his chin and kissed him before throwing myself onto the sofa, half leaning on him like a pillow, and pulled his arm around my shoulder. "What movie are we watching?"

"*Reservoir Dogs*. Classic Tarantino. Is that okay?"

I sighed, completely content and happy. "Like I said. Perfect."

THREE

I had to work, which was crap, but Andrew said he'd drive me to my client's place. I was trying not to think about how weird it might be for him, driving his boyfriend to work, where I was spending the evening pretending to be the boyfriend of someone else. I offered to call a cab, but Andrew wanted to reassure me he was okay with it.

I finished tying my bowtie, slipped on my jacket, and walked out to where Andrew was waiting.

He stared. Wide eyed, open mouthed. "Oh."

I looked down at my tuxedo. "Do I look okay?"

He cleared his throat. "Um, yes." He shook his head. "Jesus."

"It's a formal, black-tie dinner," I said, crinkling my nose. "And anyway, the suit hides my sleeves. Peter would prefer me to not show my tattoos."

Andrew scowled at that. "Did he say that?"

I tried not to smile. "I asked. It's a part of my job to look the part. Peter's a bit older and has always been vocal in his distaste of tattoos, so his ex-boyfriend would know something was up if I were to turn up with mine showing."

"Well, Peter's a bit weird."

"He's not the weirdest," I conceded. "He just likes men half his age. Nothing wrong with that. I think he was looking to settle down, but his ex wasn't ready for that."

Andrew nodded thoughtfully. "You think they'll get back together? His ex-boyfriend's name is Duncan, yes?"

"Yep. Duncan Doolittle. And I don't know if they'll get back together. Duncan's a hard one to read."

Andrew smiled. I'd told him some things about this new job, so he got the job reference. "I'm almost certain not all vets have the last name Doolittle. And couldn't you have kidnapped someone's dog to take it into his clinic? That'd have to be a bit more exciting than sitting through a formal dinner."

I chuckled at him. "Not to mention illegal. And no, Peter works with Duncan's best friend. That's how they met. So the friend will be at this dinner because it's a work thing. He'll see me with Peter and no doubt tell Duncan. Then Peter and I will take his cat, not some stolen dog, to the vets, and Doctor Dreamy Duncan Doolittle can decide if he's jealous or not."

"Doctor Dreamy Duncan Doolittle?"

"Yes. Alliteration about appearances is always awesome when articulated artistically."

Andrew laughed. "That was terrible."

"Then why did you laugh?"

He was still smiling. "I was being polite."

I rolled my eyes. "You were not. You totally think I'm great."

He didn't answer, but he also didn't stop smiling. "You look great in that tux," he said, giving me another once over. "Maybe we should go out somewhere fancy sometime so I get a night with you dressed like that too."

I lifted his hand and kissed his knuckles. "Any time. A black-tie jazz night perhaps?"

He smiled shyly. "Would you dance with me?"

"You told me you don't dance."

"I don't dance in nightclubs or bars."

"But at some fancy place dressed in a tux you would?"

"Yes."

"Then yes. On a dance floor full of elegantly dressed hetero couples in one of LA's best jazz bars? Hell yes, I would. And you"—I kissed him lightly— "would be the most dapper of them all."

"Most dapper?" He laughed. "Is that the male equivalent of Cinderella?"

"I was thinking more like James Bond, but whatever."

He chuckled and sighed happily. "Well, I still think you look great—"

"Dapper."

He snorted. "Okay. I still think you look dapper in your suit. And I'd be lying if I said I wasn't jealous."

I put my forehead to his. "If it means anything, I'd prefer to be here with you."

His blue-grey eyes flashed with a smile. "I know."

I held his chin between my thumb and forefinger. "So, what are your plans for tonight? Are you really going to go hang out here and downstairs with Emilio?"

"Would that make you insanely jealous?"

"Yes. And don't look so amused. You could at least try and look put out."

Andrew laughed. "Actually, I'm going to see my parents."

"Oh, how's Yanni going?" Yanni was the acting-student guy I'd been paid to find for my last client, who turned out to be the charming arsehole who belted the crap out of Yanni and called it love. I'd brought Yanni home with me, not really knowing what else to do with him, and Andrew had said he knew of some place where Yanni would be welcome and safe. That *place* just happened to be his parents' house. The plan was to find Yanni a flat of his own, but a week later and he was still there. Andrew hadn't mentioned him for a day or two. "Found somewhere for him to live yet?"

"No. Well, I'm sure there's been plenty of safe-houses, but to be honest, I think my mom likes having him around. Another actor in the house and she'll be in heaven. She probably has the furniture in the living room pushed to one side and has had the poor guy adlibbing scenes with her from her latest acting class." Andrew smiled fondly. "She used to make Sarah and I do that."

"Didn't want to be actors?"

He looked horrified. "Lord no. That's why I did piano and Sarah did ballet. Being on stage in front of a critical audience is my worst fear. I wouldn't even do piano recitals." He shuddered.

"Worst fear? Like ever?"

"Terrified. What's your greatest fear?"

"Being burned alive. Which is a stupid way to say it actually because you don't say drowned alive or stabbed alive. So, it's more a case of being set on fire till you're not alive anymore."

"Death by fire."

"Yes! Death by fire."

Andrew nodded slowly, his brow furrowed. "I can see why. Being on stage is a lot like death by fire. Harrowing, excruciatingly painful, torture."

I refrained from rolling my eyes. "Yeah, they're so alike."

He laughed. "Speaking of excruciatingly painful, remember how Sarah called me that time and told me we'd be invited to some fancy lunch at my parents' house?"

"Yeah."

"Well, Mom asked if you'd like to come along." Andrew bit his lip and looked to the floor. Before I could reply, he quickly added, "I told her I wasn't sure if we were up for that just yet, and now I know your worst fear, you'd probably prefer to be burned at the stake than to spend an afternoon in the company of my parents and their friends."

I put my finger to his chin and lifted his face so he'd look at me. "I'd love to. When is it?"

"Not this Sunday but the next."

"If I don't have to work, I am all yours."

"Are you sure? It'll be boring and full of people who think they're better than they are."

How could I ever refuse him when he looked at me so happy and hopeful? "Of course I'm sure. You have a toothbrush in my bathroom. I'm pretty sure that's a 'social lunch with your parents' qualifier."

He gave me a shy, half-smile. "I like having your toothbrush in my bathroom. I smile every morning when I see it." He shook his head a little and squinted his eyes closed as his skin flushed right down his neck. "God, I shouldn't have said that."

I cracked up laughing because I'd totally thought the same thing. "Don't be embarrassed. If there was a magazine titled *Things That Make Spencer Happy*, your toothbrush in my bathroom would be on the cover."

"Really?"

"Yes, really. Amongst other things, but yes, I'd have a whole cover issue dedicated to that. Right after the issue with your picture and good music, classic movies, and green tea."

Andrew chuckled and pressed his lips to mine. "Thank you."

"What for?"

"For getting me. For not thinking I'm an idiot. For doing the whole magazine cover thing, as well. I've never known anyone that does that like me. Until I met you." He pecked his lips to mine again. "And for what it's worth, if there was a magazine called *Things That Make Andrew Happy*, you'd be on the cover too."

I was grinning. I couldn't help it. "Oh, don't forget, you need to think of something to draw for my next tattoo."

He made a face. "You'll really get whatever I draw tattooed onto your body?"

"Well yeah, if I like it."

"Oh good. So no pressure or anything."

I gave him a light kiss with smiling lips. "It'll be fine. You know me better than anyone, so I'm sure whatever you come up with will be perfect."

He stared, literally stared into my eyes. "Do I?"

"Know me better than anyone?" I resisted the urge to look away but managed a nod. "Yeah." Before my chest burst with nerves, I changed the subject. "Come on, we better get going or I'll be late."

Andrew was pretty quiet in the car on the way to Peter's. I'd given him the address, which he'd promptly punched into an app on his phone and set about driving me. It wasn't an overly long trip, and when I put my hand on his thigh, he quickly slid his non-driving hand over mine. He smiled at me but didn't say much. When we drove up Peter's street and he pulled the car into the kerb, I asked, "Everything okay?"

"Yes, of course. Just thinking about what tattoo I'm supposed to draw for you."

I didn't exactly believe him. I think he was more worried about my night with Peter than he was letting on, but he just didn't want to admit it. "Don't over think it. Sometimes the best ideas are the simplest."

"Easier said than done."

"True." I looked up at Peter's house. "I better get going. Have a fun night with your parents. Tell them I'll be there next Sunday. And tell Yanni I said hi."

He almost smiled, but then his eyes darkened. "Can I kiss you?"

Oh. Random, but okay. "Anytime you want."

He leaned over the centre console and I did the same, but as our lips met, he put his hand to my face and kissed me deeper. And harder. And better. It wasn't just a quick good-night snog. It was a "you might be spending time with him but you fucking belong to me" kind of kiss. I'd never experienced possessiveness by anyone before, and I had to admit, it was hot as hell.

I pulled away with a groan. I was breathless, and my heart rate spiked. I licked my lips tasting him there. "Fuck, Andrew."

He let out a breathy laugh. "Sorry."

"Jesus. Don't apologise. You can kiss me like that anytime you want." I opened my door, but before I got out, I added, "And for what it's worth, the answer is yes, I will."

He looked confused. "Answer to what?"

"The question in that kiss. The 'you better be thinking of me tonight', which is not technically a question, but you know what I mean."

Andrew blushed which told me my assumption was correct. "Is that right?"

I leaned over the console and waited until he leaned in too. When my lips were almost touching his, I said, "Yes, I'll be thinking of you." I kissed him soft and sweet. "I'll call you," I promised and got out of the car.

He drove off, and before I'd reached Peter's front door, I shot Andrew a quick text.

Oh, btw, Possessive-Andrew can show up
anytime he likes. That kiss was hot.

I was still smiling as I knocked on Peter's door. He opened the door, clearly surprised and pleased by my appearance. "Spencer," he said, giving me another once over as I walked inside, "you look great."

"Thank you, you too."

Peter was wearing a tux like me, and he wore it well. He was a forty-three-year-old, reasonably fit-looking purchasing manager for a large corporation. He just happened to have a thing for twinks in their twenties. He claimed he liked their energy, which I assumed he meant he liked their libido and stamina. Not that that was a bad thing. Peter was a very nice, polite, and professional man. I know I'd called him old and stuffy to Andrew, but Peter wasn't that bad. I liked him. He was decidedly normal and undecidedly single after his vet boyfriend declared he didn't want the settled-down life in the 'burbs.

I felt a bit sorry for Peter. From what he told me, he'd spoiled his boyfriend with time and affection, but the guy had grown bored and called it quits. I'd done some online scouting and found his ex-boyfriend, a guy by the name of Duncan, was already out playing the field. His social media statuses and comments made no attempt at hiding his on-the-market approach to life. Peter had simply thought it might mean Duncan needed to get out a bit and party, but that he'd come back when he realised the partying lifestyle wasn't all it was cracked up to be. That was a month ago, and now it was time to see if Duncan had had his fun and wanted to get back with Peter.

Which is where I came in.

Duncan's best friend, Zach, was an IT guy at the same

company Peter worked for, and Zach was attending this work dinner tonight. The plan was, he'd see Peter with me and tell Duncan. We'd then turn up with Peter's cat at the vet clinic Duncan worked at, concerned over some non-existent problem.

That was how it was supposed to go, anyway.

"You ready to go?" he asked, looking at his watch.

I gave him a reassuring smile when he looked at me. "Let's get this show on the road."

FOUR

The dinner function was held in the grand ballroom at some fancy golf club, and we fit right in, pulling up in Peter's latest model two-door Audi. He handed the keys over to the valet and held his arm out for me to take, exactly as we'd planned.

Clearly, hiding his sexuality wasn't a consideration for Peter. He was distinguished and confident and held his chin high as he walked into a formal work dinner with a man on his arm. Every other couple I saw consisted of a man in a tux and a woman in an evening gown of some design and colour. But no one looked twice at us, except to extend a warm welcome to Peter and a polite smile to me.

He introduced me as "his friend" and after a few short pleasantries were exchanged, we were seated at a round table with six other people. Peter sat on my right, and a lovely lady by the name of Rosa sat on my left. She was the wife of an employee so, like me, she had no idea who anyone else was.

We made small talk while the room filled. When Peter put his hand on my arm and whispered, "Zach is here," I followed his line of sight and recognised the guy from photos I'd seen on Duncan's Instagram.

We watched as Zach chatted and laughed with the colleagues at his table. When he scanned the room and found Peter, and therefore me, he gave nothing away but a small smile and a nod.

Throughout the course of the night, I noticed Zach look our way a few times. He had his phone out during the night, but if he was texting Duncan, I simply couldn't say.

After the main course, I excused myself and went to the bathroom. I locked the stall door behind me and pulled out my phone. Andrew had replied to my text hours earlier.

> Possessive Andrew only comes out when he needs to. Like Bruce Banner. Only not as green.

I smiled at my phone and quickly replied.

> You can go Hulk on me anytime you like.

> Night is boring as hell. CEOs making shit speeches and telling not-funny jokes. It's painful. Rather be in bed being Hulked by you.

I slid my phone back into my pocket, flushed the toilet just for show, and went to the wash basins. Zach was waiting for me. He was a skinny guy with too much hair and long, spidery fingers. He was certainly not threatening. He seemed... nervous?

"Hey," he said.

"Hi." I proceeded to wash my hands and dry them, waiting for him to speak.

"I saw you're here with Peter?"

"Yes."

"He's a nice guy."

"He is. Do you work with him?" I asked, knowing they worked in different divisions but needing to push the conversation along.

"No, no," he said quickly. "He's um, he was seeing a friend of mine."

"Oh." I was surprised by his honesty. "Is that Duncan? He told me about the break up."

Zach nodded. "Yeah. Duncan's not a bad guy; he just graduated and started working at the clinic and has a different life now. I guess he just wanted something different? But I'm happy to see Peter with someone new, I have to say. I always liked him. He's a nice guy. Genuine, ya know? And Duncan kinda threw it in his face. I was sorry he did that."

I nodded slowly. "Peter is a good guy."

Zach stuffed his hands in his pockets. "Anyway, I just wanted to say that."

I gave him a smile. "Thanks." Seeing this as my opportunity to ask questions, just as Zach turned to leave, I said, "Um, can I ask you something?"

"Sure."

"Is Duncan interested in getting back with him?" I had to play the part. "I'm just wondering if I have competition, that's all."

Zach smiled sadly. "Nah. He's been so busy fucking everything that looks twice at him. He said he's done with monogamy—or whatever he called it—for good. I wish he wasn't—I worry about him—and Peter was so good to him." He sighed. "Duncan has a track record of leaving behind a trail of broken hearts."

It was pretty clear that Zach was one of them. "Oh."

He laughed and shook his head a little. "Yeah." Then he

brightened. "Anyway, tell Peter I said hi and that I'm glad he's moving on too."

"I will."

He turned and walked out, and I was left with the horrid task of telling my client it was game-over.

I took my seat, and Peter lifted the linen napkin from his lap and neatly folded it on the table before him. "You spoke to Zach."

"I did."

"And he told you Duncan wasn't interested in a reunion."

"He did."

Peter stared at nothing before him, then blinked a few times before nodding slowly. "I assumed as much."

"Peter," I started.

"It's fine. He always was a—" He stopped short of finishing that train of thought. "Once he made up his mind, that was it. I should have known."

Oh, man. He looked like he'd just had the wind knocked out of him. "Wanna get out of here?"

He sighed loudly, took one last look around the buzzing room, then looked at me. "Yes."

I said a quiet goodbye to Rosa, collected my jacket from the back of my chair, and waited for Peter to do the same. He never said a word to anyone except to the valet, who quickly produced his car.

"I would offer to drive," I said getting into the passenger seat, "but you don't really want me to drive your car. Steering wheel's on the wrong side of the car, for a start, not to mention driving on the wrong side of the road."

Peter almost smiled.

"I can't drive you, but I can suggest a bar that has great Scotch."

He smiled ruefully now. "I'm not one to drown myself in

sorrows and liquor. My father did enough of that for the both of us."

For whatever reason he said that, I had a feeling it was information he rarely shared. His distinguished mask had slipped a little, proof that Duncan's final rejection hit him harder than he let on. I didn't want him to be alone right now. "Let me buy you a coffee then."

He seemed to think it over for a moment before giving me a nod. "You're not letting me get out of it, are you?"

I smiled at him. "No."

We found a diner on Santa Monica Boulevard about a ten minute drive from my place, and seeing they didn't have tea on offer, I ordered two coffees. We sat in a booth seat, and it wasn't long until the waitress brought them to our table. It wasn't anything fancy, just diner coffee, straight black. "You don't like coffee," Peter said when she was gone.

I gave him a kind smile. "I'll suffer through it. Anyway, if I add enough sugar, I can't taste how horrible it is."

He laughed quietly as he absently stirred his cup, and slowly but surely, his smile faded away. "What did Zach say?"

I wasn't going to repeat the whole "fucking everything that looks twice at him" line. Peter felt like shit enough as it was. "Just said he was happy to see you were moving on. He said he wished Duncan hadn't hurt you, but he has a habit of leaving behind a trail of broken hearts."

Peter smiled ruefully. "I knew that going in. I thought I was lucky to snare him. And I thought it'd be different with me. Famous last words, huh?"

"Don't blame yourself. The fault is on him. You did nothing wrong. It just wasn't meant to be."

"Did Zach say that Duncan was happy?"

And that right there showed Peter's kindness. He just wanted to know if his ex was happy. "He is."

Peter sighed and sipped his coffee. "I thought he was happy with me. I should have known better. I mean, no young guy wants to settle down... they don't want to *settle* at all."

"Not all young guys," I amended.

"Would you want to settle down? Not with me," he added quickly. "But with your guy, what's his name?"

"Andrew."

"Would you settle for the quiet life with Andrew?"

"Two months ago I would have said no way. Hell, even one month ago, I'd have called you crazy. But now...? Well, now I'd have to say I would seriously consider it."

Peter raised his eyebrows and nodded slowly. "He must be something special."

"He is."

"And you met him when he hired you?"

I had given Peter a brief rundown of my personal life, like I did with all new clients, when he'd first hired me. "I did."

"So his ex didn't want him either," he stated, though it was more a shot at himself than at Andrew.

"Not exactly. I just helped Andrew discover he didn't really want his ex back at all."

"So, I'm your only failed statistic. That has to put a dent in your perfect success rate."

I gave him a smile. "I still consider you a success. Now you're free to move on to someone who will appreciate you for who you are."

"Did you read that on some Dr. Phil slogan?"

"Not quite." I laughed as I sipped my coffee, and Peter chuckled when I made a face.

He nodded toward my cup. "How is it?"

"Awful."

It made him smile, and I considered that a win too. My

phone buzzed in my pocket, and I pulled it out to find a message from Andrew.

> How's your night going?

"I just need to reply to this. I won't be a second," I told Peter. I didn't want him to think me rude.

> Finished, and it didn't end well. Just having commiseration coffee with Peter.

> Oh. I'm sorry.

> Where are you?

"Sorry," I said to Peter, putting my phone on the table.

"That was Andrew?" he asked. "I can tell by the smile."

I'm pretty sure I blushed. "Uh, yeah."

My phone buzzed on the table, but I ignored it. "You can answer it, Spencer. I don't mind," Peter said, sipping his coffee.

> Waiting for Yanni to come out of the Seven-Eleven on Santa Monica. He wanted root beer.

"They're actually just down the road," I told Peter as I texted out my reply to Andrew.

> We're in Ziggy's Diner, just near South Bentley.

"Tell them to join us," Peter offered.

"Nah, it's okay," I told him.

"Spencer, please. Tell them to come. Whoever *they* are."

"*They* would be Andrew and Yanni. Are you sure?"

"I wouldn't have suggested it otherwise. At any rate, the distraction would be welcome."

Fair enough, I thought. I selected Andrew's name and hit Call. He answered on the second ring. "Hey," he replied softly. "Everything okay?"

"Yeah, it's fine. Want to join us? You're not far from here, right?" Then I thought maybe Yanni might not want to. "Would Yanni be up for it?"

I heard him ask, though it was muffled. "We'll be there soon."

He hung up, and I told Peter they'd be joining us shortly. "So, I finally get to meet your Mr Wonderful."

That made me smile. "You do. Though there's something you need to know about Yanni. He's a real nice guy, but he's had a rough couple of months, so he might be a bit standoff-ish. But don't take it personally."

I didn't want to say any more than that because it wasn't my place to do so. But the truth was, I hadn't seen Yanni since we'd left him at Andrew's parents' house two weeks ago. Andrew had seen him a few times and said he was doing well but still had issues to deal with which was more than under-standable.

And when he walked in, I almost didn't recognise him. I noticed Andrew first, of course, and stood to greet him. I kissed his cheek, then turned my attention to the man behind him. Yanni looked a hundred times better than he had just two weeks before. His hair was cut and shiny, his eyes were brighter and without the darkened circles underneath them. He'd even put on a few much-needed pounds. "Yanni, you look good!"

He surprised me with a hug. "Spencer. I can't thank you enough."

Pulling back from him, I waved my hand at the table to

the seat opposite where I'd sat with Peter. "Please take a seat. Peter, this is Yanni. And this is my Andrew."

Andrew looked at me with a raised eyebrow. "*Your* Andrew?"

Wait, what? "Is that what I said?"

He laughed and waited as Yanni slid into the booth seat first. Yanni sat opposite Peter, Andrew across from me, and I ordered two more coffees.

"And pie," Andrew said.

"What kind?"

"Doesn't matter," he replied. "As long as it's pie."

Peter ordered some pie and Yanni did too, but I declined. "I can just have some of yours," I told Andrew.

"Do you think so?" he asked, almost in a challenging way. "Does the James Bond suit make you braver?" There was a playfulness in his eyes as he slid his foot alongside mine under the table and tried not to smile.

I looked down at my tux. "I thought you liked my suit."

Peter cleared his throat. "So," he said, redirecting the conversation, "you're Spencer's Andrew."

"Apparently," Andrew answered, giving him a warm smile. "Yes. I am."

"He talks a lot of you," Peter said.

Andrew looked at me and tilted his head. "Is that right?"

"Only when warranted," I declared, trying not to be too embarrassed. "Like when we were discussing people who can eat their body weight in food every day and still have the body of a god."

Andrew blushed from his neck to the tips of his ears. He cleared his throat at the same time he kicked me in the shins under the table. "I um, I spend an hour in the gym every day so I can eat what I want, like an entire piece of pie that I'm not sharing."

I laughed, despite the sting in my shin. "Yanni? How's life with the Landon's going?"

"Oh, it couldn't be better," he said. "They're just the nicest people, ever."

"But they're driving him crazy," Andrew added.

Yanni laughed and shook his head vehemently. "No, no. They've been very generous. I really do owe you everything, Spencer. If it weren't for you…"

Peter looked at me questioningly, but it was Yanni who explained. "My ex hired Spencer to track me down and… *befriend* me. He… wasn't a nice man, and Spencer took me in. He saved me."

Oh. "Well, I don't know about that. I couldn't leave you where you were, that was for certain. It was Andrew's parents who took you in." Peter was staring at me so I looked at him and said, "I kinda just did what was right."

"You're one of the good ones, Spencer," he said. Then, with a heavy sigh he gave Yanni and Andrew a sad smile. "My *ex* is exactly that. My *ex*. It was confirmed tonight that he has no interest in returning to me."

"I'm sorry to hear that," Andrew said. Yanni nodded sympathetically.

Peter simply shrugged. "Well, if he can move on so easily, it should be easy for me to do the same, right?"

"If only it was," Yanni answered quietly.

Peter smiled at him. "So very true. Anyway, Spencer here very graciously offered to keep me company, for which I'm grateful."

Just then, the waitress brought over plates of pie, saving me from further embarrassment in the form of compliments and acknowledgments. I collected my teaspoon from the side of my barely-touched coffee and tried to angle a piece of Andrew's pie. He smacked my hand away and pointed his fork at me. "Don't even try it."

I laughed, and while he was distracted by looking at me, I quickly scooped a corner of his pie onto my spoon. I shoved it in my mouth before he could argue. Andrew's mouth fell open in feigned offense, or maybe it was real, I wasn't sure. "Quality control," I told him. "I had to make sure it was fit for your consumption. You may now proceed to eat."

"I hate you," he said.

"No, you don't."

Peter and Yanni were looking at us, so I explained, "He just says that. He doesn't really mean it."

"I can see that," Peter said fondly.

I cleared my throat and sipped the putrid coffee, all the while pretending I wasn't blushing.

Andrew saved me by prompting conversation with Yanni and Peter, and when they were chatting away, Andrew eyed me and smiled. "I can't believe you ate my pie," he whispered.

"I had one bite."

"You owe me."

I quirked an eyebrow suggestively, my interest piqued. "Oh, really?"

He chuckled but didn't reply. Not that it mattered, because I already planned to take him up on whatever he wanted. Peter and Yanni were now talking about the classic movies of the silent era, debating the man that was Charlie Chaplin. It was great to see Peter smile, and Yanni was a different guy than the one I met a few weeks before.

The conversations lasted until our coffee cups were empty. Peter clapped my shoulder. "Well, I should be going. But thank you for this evening."

"No worries at all," I said, starting to slide out of the booth seat.

"If you want to catch a movie," Yanni said, "there's a cinema in West Hollywood that plays silent films." I don't think he realised how it sounded, like he'd just asked Peter out on a date.

"Oh," Peter said, clearly surprised. He swallowed hard and spoke kindly. "I'm truly flattered, but I'm not looking for that right now. I think I need to give my old heart some breathing room."

Yanni looked horrified. He paled and his mouth fell open. Not in fear, like I'd seen on him before, but in the mortified kind of way. "I didn't mean..." He shook his head and turned to Andrew for help. "I didn't mean... Oh God."

Andrew gently put his hand on Yanni's arm before he could have a meltdown of some sort, but he looked to Peter when he spoke. "I don't think Yanni meant it like a date."

Yanni shook his head again and swallowed almost violently. His eyes were wide and held a flicker of panic I'd been unfortunate enough to witness in him just two weeks before. "No, I'm so not ready for that. Like really, *really* not ready for that. But my therapist said I should try and make new friends. You like silent films, and I love them, and I just thought, well, I don't even know what I thought."

Thankfully, Peter could read the situation, and from what very little he knew of Yanni, he knew enough to tread gently. "Yanni," he said warmly. "I'd love to see a film with you. Spencer and Andrew can come along if they'd like"—he looked to me and nodded before turning back to Yanni—"if you'd prefer. Because having *friends* sounds perfect to me right now. Well, friends, popcorn, and Charlie Chaplin."

Yanni let out a breathy smile, visibly relaxing. He nodded. "Okay."

"Spencer can give you my phone number and email," Peter said to him.

"I can," I agreed. I slid out of the booth and waited for Peter to do the same.

He put his jacket back on before straightening up again. "Are you right to get a lift home with these boys?" he asked me.

"Yeah, it's fine," I told him. "Peter, I'm sorry tonight didn't go as planned."

He offered a more genuine smile and a small nod of his head. "I'll be in touch," he said. He said goodbyes to Andrew and Yanni, and when he'd walked out the door, I fell back into the seat with a sigh.

I threw my jacket on the seat beside me. "Man, I wanted him to be one of my success stories."

"He's a nice guy," Andrew offered.

"He is. Decent and honest. Which is rare these days."

"Except for me." Andrew sniffed indignantly. "I was honest and decent, right?"

I laughed. "Honest, yes. Decently indecent. In the best of ways."

Andrew threw his scrunched up napkin at my face. "Just because you're looking all hot in your tux with your bowtie off and buttons open doesn't mean you can say those things."

I looked to Yanni to tell him Andrew had a thing for James Bond, but he was biting on his bottom lip and picking at his nail. "Yanni? You okay?"

He looked up startled. "Oh, sure. Well, not really. Do you think I should have done that? Asked Peter if he wanted to be friends? I mean, who even does that outside of kindergarten? But he seems like a nice guy? Doesn't he? I know my ability to see people for what they are isn't great, but we like the same movies, don't we? No one else I know loves silent films."

He was rambling nervously, every statement sounding like a question. He was still so insecure and probably rightly so.

But he was trying. He was trying to make his life better, seeing a shrink, and seeking to broaden his social circles. He was trying to get back everything his abusive ex, arsehole boyfriend had taken away.

"I think you and Peter would be good friends," I told him. "I've only known Peter a week, but we've talked a lot. I've asked him a bunch of personal questions, and he was honest with me every time. I've been to his house, I've been in his car, and I felt 100% comfortable with him at all times."

Yanni's eyes flinched, but he nodded and took a deep breath. "Good."

"And you didn't ask him if he wanted to be friends," I added. "You asked him if he wanted to hang out sometime. And that's what new friends do. You did good."

He smiled this time, and when I glanced at Andrew, I found him staring at me with those dark, heavy-lidded, "I want to fuck you" eyes. I raised an eyebrow at him in question, but he shook his head and laughed me off. Then he straightened up and said, "We better get going. It's getting late."

I grabbed my jacket and paid the tab, and we walked out together. "Are you sure you're right to drive me home?" I asked as we made our way to Andrew's car.

Yanni stopped walking. "If you two wanna go, I can..." He looked off down the street.

Andrew sighed and looked at us both over the roof of his car. "Would you two just get in?"

Yanni opened the back door, leaving me to get in the front passenger side. "He's always bossy like that," I told him as we all got into the car. "Don't let his geeky sweater vests fool you. He was on the cover of *Bossy Geeks* and everything."

Andrew started the car and stared at me. "I hate you."

I took his hand and kissed his knuckles. "No, you don't."

I glanced back to Yanni to see him smiling at us. "You two can stop being so cute now."

"Well, Spencer can," Andrew deadpanned. "I, unfortunately, am cute all the time."

I laughed. "It's true. He is."

We dropped Yanni back to Andrew's parents' house and said a quick, quiet hello to Mrs Landon. She was up reading over some report, looking glamorous as ever, even at such a late hour. The fabric of her overshirt flowed behind her like a stage performance as she kissed Andrew's cheek, then to my surprise, she kissed mine. She noticed my half-undone tux. "It's been an eventful night," I said by way of explanation.

She smiled, seemingly delighted. "I can see that."

Andrew took my hand and pulled me back toward the car. "We'll see you at one next Sunday."

She sighed into the night, then looked at me. "Spencer, please be here at eleven. Don't let him tell you any other time."

Andrew laughed as he got into the car. I waved her off, and Andrew drove us down to the gate where he entered in the security number and proceeded out onto the street. I took his hand again and held it on my thigh. "It was nice of you to take Yanni out tonight."

"He's had two weeks of solitude and therapy, not to mention living with my parents. I just thought he needed to get out of the house."

"He's trying to get his life back on track."

Andrew nodded. "And you were great with Peter tonight. He obviously needed to talk."

"He needed to not be alone," I amended.

"And what you said to Yanni…" He looked from the road to me, then back to the road. "You're so good with people. You say all the right things to make people feel better about themselves. You don't do it to be patronising at all; you do it because you're a good person."

"I said those things to Yanni tonight because it was the truth." I remembered how Andrew looked at me, all dark eyed and sexy. "You liked me saying those things."

"I happen to find compassion and genuine empathy... appealing."

"Is that so?" I noticed then how we were not going in the right direction. "Um, are we not going to my place?"

"Nope. We're going to mine. I may not be the reason you wore that tux tonight, but I can damn well be the reason you take it off."

I grinned at him. "Mmm, Bossy Andrew. My favourite."

"I thought you liked Hulk Andrew."

"I like all the Andrews."

He laughed at that, though somewhere between then and arriving at his place, Bossy Andrew disappeared and Steamy Andrew was firmly in his place. We were no sooner inside his front door when he took my jacket and threw it carefully over the back of the sofa. He pulled me close to him, our lips almost touching, his eyes were intent, his expression serious. Without a word, he slowly unbuttoned my shirt, one torturous button at a time, and slid the white fabric off my shoulders. I let it fall to the floor, and that was when he noticed the fresh ink on my arm.

"Your new tattoo," he whispered. "Is it sore?"

"Not at all," I said gruffly. To be honest, I'd forgotten about it. *God, was that really just this morning?*

He lifted my arm and slowly pressed his lips to the tender spot and then lifted my arm even higher and proceeded to kiss down my triceps. Fuck. He made a soft whimper sound that went straight to my dick. I was already on my way to hard, and now my balls throbbed with need.

Andrew put one hand to my jaw and roughly drew me in for a kiss. Hard lips, soft tongue, and the taste of him…

Then he pulled away, leaving me wanting and desperate. He was teasing me, proving he could own my body any time he wanted. "Andrew," I murmured.

His eyes never left mine as he slowly went to his knees. And right there in his living room, he undid my suit pants, freed my aching cock, and took me into his mouth. My fingers found purchase in his hair, and he moaned around me. The sound resonated through my cock. He snaked his hands around my thighs to my arse as he took me in deep. He worked me over thoroughly, then taking me into his throat, he swallowed around me, and I came.

FIVE

I had to admit, I really liked waking up with Andrew. Not only was his bed divinely comfortable, but there was a strange comfort, a peacefulness, a safeness in knowing he was beside me.

His hand lay across my stomach as he slept soundly. I entwined my fingers with his and breathed through the warmth that seeped through my chest. Such a simple, sweet thing to do, yet holding hands in bed was incredibly intimate. It was also another first for me.

I sighed at the ceiling, content, and if I were being honest with myself, I had to admit I was a little scared. Allowing myself to be exposed and vulnerable after all these years by freely giving my heart to another person was a frightening thing. I didn't regret it, and I didn't want to walk away.

God, that was the last thing I wanted to do. But I needed to take a moment to be sure I would still be okay if Andrew decided to say goodbye.

Was I strong enough to survive him leaving me?

What would it do to me?

Would I revert to the emotional detachment I'd once lived

by? Would I be so unrecognisable to myself that I wouldn't know where to start? Does being one half of a couple mean I lose part of who I am? Or do I gain, do I learn, do I grow? Would it make me a better person, or would it devastate me completely?

Maybe the real question I should be asking is why was I thinking Andrew would want to leave me?

I wasn't sure of any of these things. What I was certain of was that I, Spencer Cohen, the guy who once swore to himself he'd never let anyone close enough to hurt him again, had done exactly that.

I was in love with Andrew.

My stupid heart went and ignored my stupid brain. And at least my stupid mouth hadn't blurted it out to him before he was ready to hear it and before I was ready to admit it. Even though I'd overheard him tell his mother he was in love with me... What did that even mean for a guy like me?

"Wanna tell me why you're trying to break my fingers?" Andrew asked, his voice croaking, thick with sleep.

I hadn't realised I was squeezing his hand. "Oh. Sorry."

I let go of his hand but he was quick to grab it back again. He put our joined hands on my chest. "What's up? You look worried."

Shit, shit, shit. "Well, I was just wondering if I knew of any tea houses that home delivered green tea this time of day. Or anytime of the day, for that matter. I'm pretty sure Zineb would laugh and call me names in Arabic if I phoned her asking for home delivery."

Andrew chuckled. He scrubbed his free hand over his face. "You can't lie for shit. That was *so* not what you were thinking. But for what it's worth, I will buy you green tea to have here. And one of those things you have on your kitchen counter. What's it called?"

"An electric kettle? Or a teapot? Because I have both."

"The kettle. But I shall buy you both." He sighed, a happy contented sound. "In lieu of the record player you bought me."

"You know, it was very strange to realise, when I first arrived in the States, that hardly anyone uses electric kettles here," I told him. "Every house in Australia has one. A kettle and a toaster. It's like a necessity. Like plates and cutlery."

"Well, that's because Australians are weird," he said with a laugh. "What time is it?"

"Half six."

"See? Weird. What kind of time telling is that?"

"Six thirty."

"Why not just say that?"

"Because it's half six," I told him.

He laughed. "Do you really say that in Australia? Because really, does that mean it's thirty minutes past six o'clock, or that it's three o'clock because technically half six is three?"

"It's not that complicated. But it means six thirty."

Andrew laughed again and shook his head. "Maybe once I've had that elective lobotomy, I'll understand it."

I gasped and grabbed him to tickle him. He yelped out a laugh and easily overthrew me, clearly so much stronger than me. He rolled me onto my back and straddled my waist while pinning my hands to my pillow. He was naked, as was I, so I scored a glorious view of his dick. Full and heavy on my stomach, his cock was pointing straight at me.

"You should work out more," Andrew joked. "Maybe then you could put up more of a fight."

I laughed, and eyeing his dick again, I licked my lips. "Who said I wanted to win?"

Smiling, his eyes flashed with heat and mischief. "Really?"

Was he asking me if I really wanted to suck his cock? "Fuck yes."

Andrew sat up straight, his cock now protruding proudly, his balls resting on my stomach. He leaned forward a little, and I licked my lips again. He inched closer, but not close enough, and even straining my neck, I couldn't reach. I let my head fall back onto my pillow. "Do you want me to beg?"

He grinned salaciously down at me and leaned his hips forward enough so the tip of his cock reached my lips. I opened my mouth and looked up at him, waiting.

"Jesus," he murmured. He rocked his hips forward and proceeded to fuck my mouth. His cock was engorged and musky and so fucking big. I tongued him, and sucked hard, cupping his balls with one hand, pumping his base with my other.

Andrew gripped the headboard and thrust a little deeper, harder, as his self-control fell apart. He grunted and groaned, and with a final shudder, he came. I swallowed around him, drinking what he gave me, and he convulsed and cried out before finally pulling away. He slumped to the side and off me, lying motionless and speechless for a moment, until he started to laugh. "God, Jesus. Spencer."

"Did you have that lobotomy already?"

He snorted. "Feels like it."

I gave my dick a squeeze and bit back a groan. Before I could do or say, anything he rolled off the bed. "Shower, breakfast, gym."

I shook my head. "No. Blowjob, shower, breakfast, and back to bed."

He stood at the foot of the bed, his cock hanging heavy and still glistening from my mouth. His body was pale and toned; his hours a week in the gym truly did him wonders.

"How about a compromise?"

"Does it involve blowjobs, showers, breakfast, and bed?"

He laughed. "We shower, we eat breakfast. I'll drop you off at home, and I'll go to the gym. I'll meet you back at the tattoo shop for Sunday morning coffee. It'll give you some time to do whatever you need to do this morning. Sound fair?"

"What happened to my blowjob?"

He grinned. "I promise you, shower and breakfast now, and then this afternoon will be the best sex you've ever had."

Well, that had my interest well and truly piqued. And my still-hard dick. "Oh, really?"

He gave me a smug, all-knowing smile as he turned and walked into his bathroom. He left the door wide open, and I heard the water turn on. Then he called out, "And I never said anything about no handjobs in the shower."

I was in that shower cubicle with him so fast, the water hadn't even had time to get wet.

I SPENT a few hours tidying up, grabbing a few groceries at the store, and doing the coffee run for our weekly ritual of Sunday morning brunch in Emilio's shop. When Andrew arrived, he was very relaxed and happy, planted himself right next to me, and spent the next hour laughing and talking bullshit with the rest of us.

He simply slotted into my life like he'd always been there, and I couldn't remember what I did with my time when I didn't know him.

After lunch, Andrew was going through my album collection for something new to listen to, and it occurred to me that I didn't know what I'd be doing in that second if he weren't there. Probably downstairs helping Emilio or at Lola and

Gabe's place annoying them. Maybe I'd be in the city people watching or at Venice Beach... But all of those paled in comparison to spending time with him.

"You're staring into space again," he said, breaking me out of my reverie. He put the album down. "Everything okay?"

"Sure. Actually, everything's great," I told him.

"But?"

"But nothing."

"Spencer, you can't lie for shit."

"I'm not lying."

He walked over to me and gently traced his thumb over my eyebrow. He smiled. "Tell me what's on your mind."

I could tell him this, yes? That's what boyfriends did, right? They talked through shit. "I can't remember what I did with my time before I met you."

Andrew blinked and his smile never faltered. "And that bothers you?"

"Well, yes. I can't be me if I'm not who I am without you."

His smile slowly slid away. "What are you saying?"

He looked like I'd slapped him, and as I replayed what I'd just said in my mind, I realised how it must have sounded to him; almost like a goodbye.

"No, no, no, That's not what I meant." I took his hand. "I meant it in a good way. I'm not good at talking about these things, so bear with me. Spending time with you is my most favourite thing. Ever. And it's all I want to do. But I can't lose me either. Does that make sense? I spent years shutting people out to protect myself. I have never doubted who I was. But then you came along, and I don't want to be just me anymore. I want to hang out with you all the time, but we shouldn't do that should we? Because if you decide to not be with me anymore, I'm not sure I'd know what to do, and that scares me. It's been just me for so long, and I knew how to deal with that. But if I had to be just me now, I'm not sure I could."

Andrew put the pad of his thumb on my lips, stopping me from rambling on any further. "Spencer," he whispered. "I'm not leaving you."

There was such sincerity in his eyes, such honesty, it took my breath away.

"But you're right," he said gently. "We should spend time apart. That's why I suggested I go to the gym this morning and you do your thing. It was just for a few hours, but still, we need to keep our old lives intact."

I nodded. "You're not mad?"

He smiled. "Not at all. The opposite, in fact. Thank you for telling me what you feel. And"—he brushed his lips to mine—"spending time with you is my favourite thing ever as well."

I wanted to tell him how I felt. I wanted to tell him so bad. The words were on the tip of my tongue, like *right there*, yet my stupid voice was nowhere to be found. My stupid heart got too big for my chest, and it got all hard to breathe as my nerves fed the butterflies in my throat. "Andrew," I choked out.

But then his lips were on mine, in a searing, mind-clearing kiss. He pushed me into my bedroom and onto my bed where he covered my body with his. Fully dressed, he settled between my legs and continued to kiss me like his very life depended on it.

He'd kissed me before, but this was different. The way he held me, the way he rocked into me and kissed me so deeply was new. It wasn't passion and need. It was emotion and longing.

No, I couldn't find the courage to tell him how I felt, but I could show him. With every touch, with every look, every kiss, I hoped like hell he could feel every word I couldn't say. And when we were naked and he was buried inside me, we made love. Soft moans and gentle strokes, deep kisses and holding hands, there was no doubt in my mind. No, he hadn't exactly told me how he felt either, but it was in his eyes. When he moved inside me, he looked right into my eyes. He never looked away, and when he climaxed inside me, I saw it. *This man, this perfect-for-me man, loves me.*

And from the look on his face, maybe he saw the same in mine. Because that afternoon in my bed, in his arms, without a word between us, I told him I loved him.

———

AFTER ANDREW HAD GONE HOME for the afternoon, I made my way back down to see Emilio. Truth be told, I missed hanging out with him, and although Andrew and I had to make ourselves spend time apart, I was happy to spend time with my mates, as well.

Emilio looked behind me. "Where's Andrew?"

"We're spending some time apart."

Emilio shot me a look. "What for?"

"So we don't overdo it," I explained. "You know, get sick of each other."

He looked amused. "How's that working out for you?"

"I'm trying to remember what I did before I met him."

Emilio laughed and waved his tattooed hand at the messy reception desk. "You did inventory and tidied up and disinfected everything."

It really was a shambles. "Point taken. I haven't helped out in a while."

"I don't expect you to."

"No, but I love doing it." I immediately started sorting

piles of papers. "And this is my point. I can't just abandon my old life because of Andrew. I want him *in* my life, not to *be* my life."

Emilio looked up from his work. "Love is a funny thing, my friend."

"Yes, it is." I just realised I'd admitted, for the first time ever, that I knew what love was. I ignored Emilio's smile and continued to tidy the desk. "Yes, it is."

As the night wore on, I called Lola and got roped into helping her during the week, and I bought dinner for Emilio and myself, laughed and chatted just like old times. I only checked my phone about three dozen times, my disappointment growing each time there was no text from Andrew.

Later that night, when I was in my bed alone, it got the better of me. I shot him a text.

> I know we're supposed to be having solo time, but my bed smells of you and I had to say goodnight.

His response was almost immediate.

> Oh thank God you texted me. I was going insane. My bed smells of you too.

I smiled at the small screen.

> I wanted to text you since the second you left.

> Me too.

> When will I see you this week?

> Tuesday night? You can teach me how to cook something else.

Sounds perfect.

My place, half six.

Are you taking the piss at my time telling skills?

Absolutely. But I'll make it up to you on Tuesday night.

Sounds promising.

JSYK, I just added tea, a kettle, and douching bulbs to my shopping list.

I burst out laughing.

Goodnight Andrew.

Sweet dreams, Spencer.

I slid my phone onto my bedside table and fell asleep with a smile on my face.

I SPENT the next two days being Lola's lackey for her on-site jobs and helping Emilio out in the shop. I cheated with a few texts to Andrew, and he called me on Monday night, just to hear my voice. Or so he said.

We were officially both emotional saps, because the sound of his voice eased something inside me the second I answered the phone.

But by Tuesday night, I was so incredibly ready to see him. How could two days seem so long? Every minute dragged like torture, but he opened the door and smiled at me and all was right with my world.

He pulled me inside by my shirt and kissed me so thoroughly, I couldn't think straight. We stumbled back until his arse hit the back of the sofa, our mouths never apart. I could feel his erection pressing against me. I could feel his need, the urgency in his touch.

I broke the kiss to breathe. Between his scent, his kiss, and the lack of oxygen, my head was starting to spin. "Hi," I said, out of breath.

His lips were plump and wet. "Hi." His breath was sweet and warm, and his cock was hot and hard. "Sarah will be here soon," he said. "She's not staying. Just needs to collect something. Fuck, I've missed you."

I barked out a laugh. "I've missed you too." I pulled our hips together, rubbing against his hard-on. He moaned and bucked against me. Jesus, he was desperate. "How long have we got before she gets here?"

Andrew slid his hand between us and undid his fly. "Not long." He reached inside his briefs and pulled out his cock. To say I was surprised at how brazen he was being was an understatement. "Please, Spencer. I'm about to come." He put his free hand on my shoulder and urged me down. I went to my knees willingly, and the second I took him into my mouth, Andrew fisted my hair and guided me. He was in complete control, and I simply closed my eyes and opened my throat.

By the time his sister arrived, Andrew was relaxed with a smug smile and glassy eyes. "Oh, God," Sarah waved her hands in front of her face. "I can smell the testosterone and pheromones in here," she said.

I couldn't help but laugh, and she greeted me with a smile and a kiss to my cheek. "Spencer, I take it you're the reason for the look on my brother's face." She collected a box from the sofa, which I hadn't even noticed, and said, "Can't stay. Have fun, though I can tell you already have. See you both on Sunday." She kissed Andrew on the cheek, waved to me, and was gone as quick as she arrived.

Andrew locked the door behind her and said, "She's going to Mom and Dad's and wanted some of my old books to take to Yanni." Then he walked slowly over to me. "I probably should apologise about before. I've done nothing but think about you for two days, and I was a little turned on."

I put my hand to his face and kissed him softly. "Just a little?"

He smiled, but his eyes were intense and full of fire. "Now it's your turn." He gently pushed me backwards until I sat on the sofa.

"Aren't we supposed to be cooking dinner?" I asked.

He knelt between my legs, undid my zipper, and licked his lips. "We are. This is the first course. Then we cook, then you rim me, then you fuck me."

Oh, yeah. Bossy Andrew was back. His words went straight to my cock. "Have I ever told you that it turns me on when you say filthy things like that?"

He smiled. A faint blush coloured his cheeks. He freed my erection, and I put my hand to his jaw as he took me in. I thumbed his lip as I slid into his mouth, and his cheeks hollowed as he sucked me. He'd quite often pulled my hair when I blew him, and I wondered if he'd like me to do the same. I slid my hand into his short, spikey hair and fisted it the best I could.

He moaned and sucked harder.

Fuck.

"Yeah, you like that," I said, my voice gruff and harsh. I pulled on his hair again and elicited the same reaction from him. He took me deeper and swallowed around me, sucking my orgasm from me. I came down his throat, wave after wave of pleasure rolled through me. My blood warmed in my veins, and my balls ached in the best possible way.

Andrew pulled off me, and I lifted his face for a kiss. He leaned against my chest, and I slumped into the sofa. "Wow."

Andrew hummed a contented response and looked up at me. "I think we're ready for food now."

I laughed. "You're insatiable. Sex, food, sex, food."

He got to his feet and pulled me to mine, and I quickly tucked myself back in and made myself presentable. I was a little dizzy, and Andrew smiled at me. "I also enjoy music and conversation. So, how about you select some music. I'll get the dinner ingredients out of the fridge and tell you all about my day. How does that sound?"

I pulled his chin between my thumb and finger and drew him in for a smiley-kiss. "Sounds like you're a bossy shit."

Andrew just smiled and walked into the kitchen. I heard the fridge open and the rustle of bags. "I hope steak and salad sounds okay. I googled *easiest dinners to cook at home* and thought it sounded best. Oh, you'll never guess what happened at work today," he said. "It was so funny... Have you picked some music yet?"

The truth was, I was still standing exactly where he'd left me, smiling like an idiot. "Just looking now." I went over to his record player and saw some records he didn't have last time I was here. "Hey, you never told me you got this one?"

I turned to find him at the doorway that leads to the kitchen, wiping his hands on a dishtowel. "Oh yeah, I picked it up yesterday. And I got the *Best of Australian 80s* for you. Wasn't sure if it was your thing, but I saw it and it made me think of you, so yeah, I got it." He blushed a little, which was all part of the paradox that was Andrew Landon. He could demand me to get on my knees and suck his dick without batting an eyelid, yet he'd blush at the most innocent of things.

"It's really great," I told him. "Thank you." I slid the album out of its sleeve and put it carefully onto the turntable and lowered the tonearm. I walked straight over to Andrew and kissed him soundly. "You're remarkable." He blinked and straightened his sweater vest like he was trying to brush off my compliment. I lifted his chin so he looked directly into my eyes. "You're a remarkable man, Andrew. Now, about that steak…"

We cut salad and cooked steak, all while Andrew recounted his day at work. I laughed as he told me the story that had him and Shell in stitches, and he listened intently as I told him how Lola did the makeup for a marketing photo-shoot while I handed her brushes and palettes like a nurse hands a surgeon scalpels. He didn't believe me that there are over a hundred shades of pink, and not only did Lola have them all, but I could almost discern the difference between *Ego* and *Swish*, and I was now considered an expert in kabuki brushes.

After dinner we planted ourselves in front of the TV for a while, watching Jeopardy. I was leaning back and Andrew was half laying on me with our hands entwined on his chest as we tried to outdo each other with correct answers.

When the show cut to an ad break, like I was a contestant on Jeopardy, I said, "I'd like to choose my favourite subject, thanks, Alec."

Andrew chuckled and played along. "And that is?"

"Andrew."

He squeezed my hand. "Okay, first clue. Andrew's—"

I pressed down on his chest like it was a buzzer. "Bzzzz. What is nine inches?"

He laughed. "Correct."

"Have you really ever measured it?"

"Veto."

"So that's a yes."

"No."

I laughed. "Next clue."

"Will you interrupt this one?"

"Yes."

He chuckled. "Andrew's favourite—"

I used his chest as a buzzer again. "Bzzzz. What is sex and food? And music and conversation, but mostly sex and food."

He laughed, vibrating against my chest. "Correct."

"I'm good at this game."

Andrew snorted before he gave another clue. "Andrew said we'd be doing this tonight."

"Bzzzz." I buzzered him again. "What is rimming and fucking?"

He burst out laughing and got up. He held his hand out for me and pulled me to my feet. "Correct again. You are tonight's winner. Want to collect your prize?"

Keeping hold of his hand, I led him upstairs. "Hell yes, I do."

"Look at your smile," Lola said. She and Daniela were taking the piss out of me. I'd been wearing one of those *ridiculous smiles* again, apparently.

"I'm not saying anything that will only incriminate me further." I walked to the door. "I'm doing a coffee run. Speak now or forever hold your peace."

Emilio grabbed his junk.

"Not that piece."

"Oh," he said, laughing me off. "Coffee would be great."

I held my hand out for Lola. "My fair lady, care to accompany me?"

"Will you give me all the dirty details?"

"Absolutely not. A gentleman doesn't kiss and tell. Or have fantastic sex, rim jobs, and blowjobs and tell, as the case might be."

Emilio put his hands over his ears. "Oh man, la la la la la." Daniela clapped her hands together and laughed, and Lola grinned as she skipped over to me and slipped her hand through my arm. We laughed all the way to the café.

FRIDAY NIGHT COULDN'T COME QUICK ENOUGH. I hadn't seen Andrew since Tuesday night. We spoke every night on the phone and we texted each other often, but I hadn't touched him, kissed him, or felt him against me in three days.

It was officially ridiculous.

I loved spending time with my friends. *Loved it.* But when I thought about Andrew, I got that giddy, jittery-butterflies kind of feeling. He made my heart lose rhythm—when his name flashed up on my phone, the sound of his voice, the buzz of my phone knowing it was a message from him. My stupid heart tripped over in my chest.

It was kind of wonderful.

Our plan was to spend Friday night and Saturday morning together, then do our own thing on Saturday night, like spend time with our friends. Then we'd do the lunch date at his parents' place on Sunday.

I was ready to throw those plans out the window the second I saw him on Friday afternoon. He was early, and I was in the cubicle Daniela used for piercings, helping her with inventory when he poked his head around the curtain.

"Hey."

I was literally stuck for words. The mere sight of him made me lose track of all coherent thought and social graces because as soon as my stupid brain registered seeing him, I tossed my spreadsheet, and in three strides I had my hands on his face and was kissing him.

He laughed against my mouth. "I hope you don't greet everyone like that."

I pulled back and slid one arm around him instead. "Not *every*one."

He laughed and waved a hello at Daniela. "Sorry to interrupt."

She had picked up my discarded paperwork, putting it back together with a smile. She looked fondly at me. "It's hard to be pissed at him when he looks so happy, yes?"

I rolled my eyes, and keeping him against me, I pushed him toward the back door. "See you guys later," I called out. "We'll just be going now."

Andrew chuckled as we made it outside, and leaving me behind, he took the stairs two at a time up to my flat. He turned and looked down at me. "What are you waiting for?"

"Just watching your arse as you climb those stairs. You really do fill out those work pants so very well."

He grinned. "Wanna know what else I fill in very well?"

I took the stairs slowly, our gazes never breaking. "What's that?" I asked, though I was pretty sure I knew what he meant. I wanted to hear him say it.

I reached the top of the stairs, and he leaned his back against my door. He bit his lip and his cheeks flushed, but his eyes were full of fire and promise. "You. I fill you up, very well."

Fuck.

I put my key into the lock, almost pressing against him,

and opened the door. Andrew walked backwards into my flat, and no sooner had I stepped inside did he push the door shut behind me and push me against it. He was all hard muscles and warm and strong, he smelled divine, and he was already hard. "I want to fill you, right now."

My moan was cut short by his mouth covering mine. He ground his hips into mine and kissed me hard, all clashing teeth and tongues and urgent hands.

I tried to pull his vest over his head, needing to feel the warmth of his skin against me, but he had other ideas. Bossy Andrew was in charge, there was no doubt about it. He batted my hands away only to drag me into the bedroom where he stripped me, stretched me, and just like he said he would, he filled me.

LATER, when we were splayed out on my bed, puffing, and boneless, he took my hand. "You okay?"

"Very."

He chuckled, still trying to catch his breath. "Wow."

I brought our joined hands to my lips and kissed the back of his hand. "I know, right? You left work early?"

"Yep. I've worked through enough lunch breaks for my boss not to care when I asked if it was okay."

"Couldn't wait, huh?"

He turned his head and looked right at me. "Nope."

"And it's still early enough that we can go out for dinner."

"Really?"

"Yep. Like a proper date kind of dinner, and if you promise to fuck me like that again later, I'll even take you to a jazz bar after we eat."

He laughed. "Or we could just stay in."

"Or we could just go out for dinner."

"Is this you being bossy?"

"Yep."

"It needs work."

"Shut up and get dressed."

He laughed. "That's much better."

SIX

Saturday morning consisted of showers and ending up back in bed. My arse was tender from the night before, and Andrew offered himself, but it wasn't what I wanted. I lay over Andrew, nestled between his thighs, our erections pressing together, but it wasn't hurried or desperate. It was slow rocking and gentle kisses, tight embraces and soft whimpers, a physical display of words I couldn't say.

It was mid-morning and we were downstairs in the shop when Andrew's friends Shell and Wendy arrived for their tattoo appointments. Both were excited, and Andrew greeted them both with a kiss to the cheek. "You guys ready?" he asked.

"Yes!" Shell said. "Oh, Spencer, hi! I take it you didn't mind Andrew leaving work early yesterday?"

I gave her a warm, honest smile. "Not at all."

"Ugh, don't start them," Emilio said with a laugh. "They're like rabbits."

I thought Andrew might have been a little embarrassed or even horribly mortified, but instead he laughed. Shell nudged him with her elbow. "You still coming out this afternoon?

Everyone'll be there. Or have you had a better offer?" She looked pointedly at me.

Andrew's smile faltered just a little. "Of course I'll be there."

I didn't miss the flicker of uncertainty that crossed his features and made a mental note to ask him about it later. Did he not want to go out with his friends? It was his idea, wasn't it? He was the one who said we should spend one afternoon this weekend apart—

"Who's first?" Emilio asked, breaking me out of my mental headspace.

"Me!" Shell said. She took a seat on Emilio's work chair, and Wendy held her hand. Andrew stood and watched, fascinated, as Emilio worked. When Shell was done and Wendy took her place, I pulled Andrew aside.

"Can we talk a minute?"

His eyes widened, and he licked his lips nervously. "Sure."

I led him out the back door, keeping it propped open so we could go back in. Andrew wiped his hands down his thighs and was a shade of pale. "You okay?" I asked.

"Um, no conversation between couples that starts with 'we need to talk' ever ends well."

A bubble of laughter escaped me, which I quickly realised was not the correct response. I snatched up his hand and pulled him in close. I stared into his eyes, now very serious. "Don't think for one second that I'd want to have that conversation with you. Please, Andrew," I whispered. I didn't trust my voice not to crack. "You won't ever hear that conversation from me."

His eyes looked such a bright blue in the sunlight. "Then what?"

"Before, when Shell mentioned going out, you looked at

her funny," I said, squeezing his hand. "Wanna tell me what that was about?"

He opened and closed his mouth a few times. "It was nothing."

I nodded slowly before I gave him a smile. "Andrew, remember when we first got together, that time in the cab you tried to shut me out and I had to go mow you down, and I told you that the whole miscommunication trope just pisses me off? You remember?"

He nodded.

"See, when we're in bed, we have no problem in saying exactly what we want, but out of it, I think we struggle. I know it's not easy for you to talk about stuff, and believe me, I am no expert. I am clueless when it comes to relationships. But I know that communication and honesty are everything."

He blinked, and dear God, he still looked like I was about to say goodbye.

I kissed him softly. "I'm not going anywhere. Are you?"

He shook his head, almost violently. "No."

"Then tell me, why the hurt on your face when Shell mentioned tonight. It was your idea, was it not?"

Andrew looked to the ground and nodded. "It was. I just..."

"You just what?"

"It's not that I don't want to go out with my friends, because I do. It's that I want you to come with me. I want you to meet all of my friends, but you said we were supposed to be taking it slow. You said we needed to spend time with our friends by ourselves."

"Which you agreed to."

"I did, but only because I thought it was what you wanted. Small steps, you said, and meeting friends and family is not small steps. I'm trying to slow down, but Jesus, Spencer, I don't want to. I know that's scary and wrong, especially after Eli, because Lord knows I rushed into everything with him and look where that got me. I don't want us to crash and burn, but—"

"Breathe Andrew," I whispered.

He took in a deep breath. "I don't want to scare you off, and I feel like I'm trying too hard."

"I've already met your family. And Shell and Wendy."

"I know." He ran his hand through his hair. "I ruined everything again, didn't I?"

I chuckled and lifted his chin so I could kiss him softly. "Not at all. But if you want me to meet all your friends, then I will."

"I come here and hang out with your friends, and they're great, they really are. But I want you to meet my crew, and I want you to like them as much as I like your friends." He sighed and frowned. "Eli refused to hang out with my friends, and I felt torn between him and them, and I don't want that to happen with you."

And there it was. The *real* reason.

I put my forehead to his. "Thank you," I whispered against his cheek. "Thank you for telling me the truth."

He mumbled, "I feel stupid."

"Don't ever discount the way you feel."

He sighed, his eyes closed. "You don't have to come with us today, but soon, if that's okay?"

"What are you guys doing tonight?"

"Going to Universal. There's a new special effects show, and we're all visual animators, which is probably kinda lame, but it's what we do. And there's a great restaurant on the City-Walk which we love. We can just organise something else for another weekend, if you want."

A slow smile crept over my face. "Are you kidding? That sounds awesome!"

His gaze shot to mine, and his lips twitched upwards. "Really?"

"Hell, yes. Would your friends mind if I tagged along?"

"Not at all. Actually, I'm pretty sure a few of them think you don't exist, so it might shut them up." His whole face was lit up; his eyes sparkled with happiness.

I laughed and lifted his chin again so I could press my lips to his. "And for what it's worth, trying to take things slow with you is like trying to hold back the tide."

"Oh, would you two get a room," Lola said from inside the shop.

Andrew and I broke apart. All smiles and holding hands, we went back in, pulling the door closed behind us. "I didn't know you were here," I said to Lola, giving her a kiss on the cheek.

"Just got in," she said, looking as gorgeous as ever. "You still coming around for dinner tonight? I told Gabe; he was finishing around five today so I thought I'd come in and get stuff organised for tomorrow. Sunday weddings are great, but breakfast weddings? Who does that? Anyway, I can't have a late one. Gotta be up early."

The corner of my mouth pulled down. Shit. "Oh. Well, actually, there's been a change of plans. I was gonna meet Andrew's crew tonight. Sorry."

"Oh," she said, giving us a stilted smile. "That's cool."

"You could come with us?" I blurted out. "Everyone can come, yeah?" I asked Andrew.

He blinked, clearly surprised. "Uh, sure."

"Is that okay?" I pressed. "You can say no. But I figure in for a penny, in for a pound, right? If I'm going to meet all your friends, they can meet mine?"

Andrew nodded, unable to stop the grin from spreading wider still.

"Hey, Emilio?" I called out.

"Yeah?"

"You free tonight?"

"Uh," he paused. "Finish at six. Wassup?"

We walked out to where he was finishing up Wendy's Peter Pan tattoo. "Universal Studio's have some new 3D drawing thing, dinner and drinks."

He shrugged. "Sounds cool. I'll ask the boss."

His one and only boss was his beautiful wife. When Emilio was finishing up, he called Daniela, she agreed, and so it was done. My closest friends were about to spend a night out with Andrew's friends.

Andrew was buzzing, excitement pouring off him. "In for a penny."

I squeezed his hand. "In for a pound."

SHOWERED, beard trimmed, hair styled for the hundredth time, I walked out dressed in tan pants, a white button-down shirt rolled to my elbows, and my blue loafers, which matched my blue suspenders. Andrew's mouth fell open when he saw me. "Too much?" I asked.

He shook his head. "Perfect."

"I'm nervous."

"Don't be. They'll love you."

The *L* word made my heart stumble in my chest. I breathed out as steadily as I could manage. It wasn't like he said it to me, but it still made me hope. *Hope?* Shit. I brushed down my shirt, and before my nerves could get the better of me, my phone buzzed. "Emilio and Daniela are downstairs. Right then. We ready?"

Andrew, dressed in his black jeans and grey argyle sweater, nodded. "Yep."

Emilio looked sharp in his designer jeans, crisp black button up shirt, and boots. Daniela looked amazing in a knee-length red dress that perfectly matched the colour of her lips. Her long black hair in waves down her back and with the flow of her dress, she could have been a Spanish dancer. It wasn't overdone; it was understated and elegant.

"Wow," Andrew said, beating me to it. "You guys look great."

"If there was a magazine called *Sexiest Latino Couple*, you guys'd be on the cover."

Emilio snorted out a laugh, but he only had eyes for Daniela. "My bride steals the show."

She looked at him fondly before saying, "We don't get out often. It's nice to get dressed up. And you two look so sweet!"

Andrew rolled his eyes, his ability to take a compliment still sorely lacking. "We ready?"

We climbed into Andrew's car and made our way toward Universal Studios. "Lola and Gabe are meeting us there," I announced to Emilio and Daniela in the backseat. "They'll have to leave early."

Andrew added, "Yanni and Peter are meeting us there as well."

This was news to me. "Oh?"

Andrew gave me a smile. "Yeah, just as friends. They actually get on really well, but that's all there is to it apparently. Or so Yanni said."

"Well, I'm glad."

"And Yanni needs to get out more. He's kinda cool. I like him," Andrew said as he drove. "He needs to meet new people, so I suggested he come along tonight as well. Hope you don't mind?"

Actually, I was happy that Andrew and Yanni had become friends. I took Andrew's hand and gave it a squeeze. "Not at all."

Andrew knew where he was going without any assistance whatsoever. As we parked and walked through the Studios, the sky was putting on a show of darkening purples that were slowly fading to black. But the night was clear and warm with crowds of happy, laughing people, and the nerves in my stomach now mixed with keen anticipation.

I wanted to meet the people Andrew called his friends. I wanted to be a part of his life, and I didn't want him to have to separate parts of himself. He shouldn't have to choose between me and his friends, and the fact his ex-boyfriend had made him do exactly that made me want to meet his friends even more.

I just hoped they liked me.

We rounded a building and a group of about six or seven people were standing around. I noticed Shell and Wendy first, then someone saw Andrew. "Hey! Here he is!"

Andrew laughed and squeezed my hand before dropping it to give his friends a hug. "Hey." He stood back. "Everyone, this is Spencer. Spencer, this is everyone. You've met Shell and Wendy," then he rattled off eight other names like Steven, Jace, Lien, Yushi... God, I was never going to remember them all.

But everyone smiled and said warm hellos. I introduced Emilio and Daniela, just as Lola and Gabe turned up. Lola wore a rockabilly-style dress with watermelons printed on it, green pumps that matched her dress, and her pink hair was coiffed perfectly in her usual 50s-style victory rolls. She looked...

"You look delicious," Andrew said.

She laughed and kissed his cheek. "Not too much?"

"Never," he said warmly, introducing her and Gabe to his friends. If our tattooed-covered bodies alarmed any of them, they never showed it.

Yanni and Peter arrived next. Yanni greeted me with a half-hug and a smile that told me he was nervous but equally brave. "Glad you could make it," I told him. Then I shook Peter's hand. "Good to see you again."

There were fourteen of us all up, and we looked like someone combined the invitations to a chess tournament and a tattoo convention. We were a mixed bunch that was for certain, but funnily enough, as we strolled through the paved alleys of Universal Studios, we all chatted and laughed.

And Andrew beamed.

The new animation show was incredible. Andrew and his friends got more out of it, on a professional level, than I ever could, but Emilio did too. When it was over, he walked in amongst Andrew and his friends talking about movement and dimension, shadowing and lines. Daniela slipped her arm through mine as we walked behind them, both of us smiling.

About halfway up the CityWalk, at a particular restaurant, they stopped walking. There were tables out the front and we pulled a few together to fit all of us, and along with our drinks, the waiter dropped off wads of paper and pencils.

I looked at Andrew. "Um, colouring in contest?"

He laughed at me. "No. They hold drawing contests. It's like a novelty restaurant."

I looked up at the name in neon lights. *Draw Me Inn*. "Are you kidding me? I can see why you like it."

He chuckled and picked up a notepad of paper. "We usually work in teams."

"Oh, hell no," I said. "I can't even draw stick figures, and you guys are all artists."

Emilio laughed and clapped his tattooed hands together. "Ah, finally something I can win at."

I pointed around the table. "They're all visual animators!"

Emilio grinned. "Don't underestimate me, brother."

Our food came, and the more we ate and drank, the more we drew and laughed. For my first attempt, I had to draw, and Andrew had to try and guess what it was. "What the hell is that?" he cried.

"Shut up! I can't draw!" I laughed.

Andrew shook his head, flustered, but needed to guess before the few seconds ran out. "Um, God. A UFO trying to tractor-beam up two frying pans."

Everyone roared laughing, and I buried my face in my hands. "It's a bicycle!"

Andrew tilted his head and squinted at my drawing. "Oh."

Emilio just about busted something, he was laughing so hard. "Okay, our turn." Emilio read the prompt card, and Peter flipped the thirty-second eggtimer. He fluidly scribbled over the pad while Daniela looked on; her smile was beautiful.

"Statue of Liberty," she said. He wasn't even finished, but even in the few pencil strokes, the outline was easy to see. Perfectly proportioned, expertly done.

"Very cool," one of Andrew's friends said, nodding his head. Was it Steven?

After a while, we stopped using prompt cards and just called out random items. When the word dragon was said, everyone smiled. Andrew quickly outlined Toothless, as did a few other of his friends. Some drew other dragons from the movie, and they were all done with incredible likeness to the real thing. Then I realised they *were* the real thing, and I couldn't believe just how incredible it really was. These people were the actual drawers of these characters, and it blew my mind how they came to life on scrap paper around the table.

After a few minutes of drawing, Lola and Gabe put in something that resembled a dog breathing fire; Yanni and Peter's dragon looked like a duck breathing fire. I didn't even attempt it, quite content to rest my hand on Andrew's thigh and watch him recreate his favourite character in front of my eyes.

But then Emilio put his pencil down and pushed his pad of paper out for all to see.

"Oh wow. That's amazing." Other praises chorused around the table, and it was easy to see why.

Emilio's dragon was no cartoon character. It was a life-like, perfectly drawn dragon, scales, teeth and tail, and gleaming eyes with its front foot clawing an egg. Even though it took him mere minutes to draw, it was good enough to be tattooed just as it was.

Everyone threw in their pencils and declared Emilio the winner. He laughed, pride and embarrassment colouring his cheeks. I think it was the first time I'd ever seen him blush.

It was getting late though, and Gabe and Lola soon stood and made their apologies for leaving early. Emilio and Daniela scored a lift home with them, though they told me in no uncertain terms we were both required for our usual Sunday morning brunch. "Um, we're busy tomorrow morning," I told them. "Early lunch at Andrew's parents." I felt bad because we never missed our Sunday coffee and tea sessions.

Emilio simply shrugged. "Then we'll make it dinner."

When they'd left, Andrew put his hand on my thigh. "You okay?"

"I am." I was smiling at him. "Your friends are pretty great."

The grin he gave me made my heart squeeze. "Thanks."

"So, Spencer," Lien said cheerfully. She was a small Chinese girl, whose huge laugh made up for her lack of height. "You're not a figment of Andrew's imagination."

Andrew groaned, and I laughed. "Nope. Real as I sit here."

"You have to admit you sounded too good to be true," Jace said with a wicked smile. "Andrew told us his new guy was this tall Australian, sweet, funny"—he batted his eyelids—"dreamy."

Andrew cleared his throat. "I didn't do the eyelid thing."

Shell came to his defence. Kind of. "Even after I'd met you, Spencer, these guys just thought I was in on the whole Andrew's-fake-boyfriend scheme."

Fake boyfriends...

I laughed. *God, if only they knew.* Well, Shell *did* know, and the wink she gave Andrew was hardly discreet. Peter and Yanni looked on amused and thankfully remained silent. "I am flattered." I smiled at Andrew, knowing my embarrassment was evident on my cheeks. "But yes, I'm real."

"Oh, I can tell," Yushi said. Her eyes danced with humour, though she clearly looked at Andrew fondly. "The way you two look at each other. Can't fake that."

I'm pretty sure I went bright red from my scalp to my toes. I tried to hide it by taking a sip of my drink, but that didn't work. I looked at Andrew, and he was as embarrassed as me. He ducked his face into my shoulder, and thankfully Peter spoke up before either of us could die of a severe case of mortification. He asked about the latest something or other which caused a friendly debate around the table of cartoonographers, Andrew included. I glanced at Peter, and he gave me a knowing nod. I smiled at him, the both of us quite content to sit back and enjoy the banter and laughter.

I was just happy to see Andrew in his element. By the time we called it a night, he was grinning from ear to ear. "My sides hurt from laughing," he said, as we crawled into bed.

"Your friends are pretty cool."

"They think you're great."

"And now they know I actually exist."

He snorted out a laugh. "I think I made you out to be too good to be true. You know, the perfect boyfriend. They thought I was full of shit."

"But I am the perfect boyfriend."

He laughed and rolled on top of me. "Yes, you are. And now they know that."

I kissed him and ran my hands down his back, over the swell of his arse, and squeezed. It made him moan into my mouth and lift his arse for more. So, being the perfect boyfriend that I was, I gave him everything he begged me for.

SEVEN

Showered, hair brushed, and stomach butterflies in full flight, I got dressed and walked out to where Andrew was sitting at his piano. He stopped playing when he saw me. I wore my tan pants, a white shirt, and blue jacket. I looked down at my outfit. "This okay?"

He stood up from his seat and very deliberately looked me up and down. "Perfect."

He wore charcoal pants I'd never seen on him before. They looked like they were tailored—the way they fit snug across his hips and thighs couldn't have been an off-the-rack fluke. A simple T-shirt complimented the pale blue lines in his grey argyle vest.

I held out my arms. "Sleeves up or down?" I wasn't sure what his parents would prefer their friends to see.

He didn't hesitate. "Up." When I was done rolling my sleeves to my elbows, he studied me for a long moment. "You look nervous."

"Because I am nervous."

"You've done a tonne of these things," he said, fighting a

smile. "Haven't you? You know, on fake dates or gala events you didn't really want to attend."

"Those are different. Those are acting, kind of. This is not. This is real. And it's your parents and their friends."

"And you, me, and Sarah will be bored out of our brains together while my parents and their actor friends recap glory days and funny stories of backstage debauchery, not their own of course, all while trying to look classier than they really are."

That made me laugh. "Okay then. Maybe we should have a code for immediate rescue. Like if I'm talking to someone and need saving, I'll pull on my beard"—I pulled the whiskers on my chin—"and you and Sarah can come save me."

Andrew grinned. "We already have codes in place. If Sarah plays with her earring, I need to bail her out. If someone insists I play the piano, I fake a cough and Sarah takes me into the kitchen to get a glass of water. Then we hide in the kitchen with the wait staff and eat all the canapés." He nodded cheerfully. "Believe me, we've been doing this since we could walk. But I will inform Sarah of the beard manoeuvre."

"Good."

"You ready?"

"As I'll ever be."

He leaned in and kissed me. "Thank you for coming with me."

"You're more than welcome."

THE LUNCH WASN'T ANYWHERE NEAR as bad as Andrew made it out to be. Actually, it was kind of fun. I had no clue who any of the guests were; famous Broadway actors or not, I'd never laid eyes on them. That worked in my favour because I had no idea who was more famous than the next person, and I met and spoke to everyone on equal footing.

It was easy to tell who thought they were more special than everyone else, and it was also very easy to see that Andrew's parents' mere presence commanded the most respect out of everyone else. I was adept at reading people, and I knew without even trying that every single person knew where Helen and Allan Landon were at all times.

They were very well respected and admired, yet so very down to earth. I had to wonder if that was why people loved them. Andrew and Sarah were funny though. They worked well as a team, dodging some guests, smiling politely at others. Years of being privy to these parties had taught them who was genuine and who was here merely to keep up appearances.

"Ugh, Gwendoline's here," Sarah whispered, hiding her mouth behind a glass of champagne.

Andrew scanned the room with covert ops precision but couldn't suppress the groan when he saw the woman Sarah mentioned.

"Who's Gwendoline?" I asked quietly.

Sarah spoke like a ventriloquist. It really was remarkable how these two had this routine down pat. "The woman by the door."

I didn't turn around, sipping my drink instead, trying to be as discreet as they were.

Then Andrew said, "The one with the mouth like a cat's ass."

I snorted champagne up my nose.

Sarah coughed back a laugh. "Well, put it this way. If she

got a role as an Egyptian mummy, swathed in gold and embalmed, she wouldn't need props or makeup."

Dabbing my nose with a napkin, I risked a glance and found the woman in question. Both Sarah and Andrew's description was absurdly accurate. Wow.

Andrew added, "I'm sure she's been dead since the 90s. Her body is running purely on the chemicals in tanning lotion and hairspray."

I was fascinated. "Well, I should go introduce myself," I announced.

"You what?" Andrew whisper-shouted. "She's creepy. She was creepy when I was five. She's creepy now."

I chuckled. "I need to see with my own two eyes if her own skin is really that leathered or if she's wearing a skin suit, like in *Silence of the Lambs*."

He laughed and mimicked the film. "'It rubs the lotion on its skin'."

"'Or it gets the hose again'," I finished with a grin.

Sarah laughed. "Oh God. You two really are perfect for each other."

So, off I went and introduced myself to Gwendoline. As it turned out, I quickly deduced she didn't socialise much anymore because in ten minutes, I had her life story and what could only be described as a well-rehearsed list of stage performances. She spoke too loudly and her eyes were unfocused, but she was clearly far too vain to wear hearing aids or glasses. Shame really, because if she could actually see what she was wearing, she'd probably be horrified. Garishly outdated and infused with mothballs and lavender, she looked as good as she smelled.

"My first production was in 1948," she told me.

Jesus Christ. I think Andrew might have been right. I

patted her arm. "Were you carried on stage as a newborn?" I laid on the charm. "You look far too young to have been cast."

"Oh, aren't you a devil?" she cooed, smiling wistfully.

I slipped her hand onto my arm and led her toward the main crowd. "Let's get you another drink," I said. We found ourselves in a group of other guests, most were easily twice my age and half the age of Gwendoline. But we mingled and chatted politely with other guests, and we laughed because Gwendoline was funny as hell. When I scanned the room, I found Andrew and his mother both smiling fondly at me. Helen breezed over to me in that graceful, elegant way she did. "Spencer, may I have a moment?"

"Of course," I answered. I offered to help Gwendoline onto a sofa, and when she was comfortable, I followed Andrew and his parents into the kitchen. There was a bunch of hired staff, all busy getting trays of canapés ready. I had no idea what this was about. Maybe they thought they were saving me from the sun-dried dinosaur in paisley purple polyester. "Gwendoline is a hoot," I told them. "Three hundred years old, perverted, and very funny."

Andrew laughed and slid his arm around my waist, but he looked to his mother. "Mom, what's up?"

Okay, so Andrew didn't know about this either.

"Spencer, I have a favour to ask you," she said softly. "I know this is probably asking too much, but considering you found Yanni—"

"What's wrong with Yanni?" Andrew interrupted. "We saw him last night and he was fine. Better than fine actually. He looked happy. I just assumed he was in his room." Andrew looked at me for confirmation.

I nodded. "He was great last night. Is he okay? And it's fine Mrs Landon. Whatever you need, just ask."

She smiled at us both. "Yanni's fine. He's chosen to spend

the afternoon with Peter. There was some silent film playing, and he didn't fancy two days in a row of crowds."

I was relieved to hear Yanni was fine, but Mrs Landon had mentioned how I'd found him. "What can I help you with?"

"Part of the Acacia Foundation is to give LGBTIQ abuse-survivors safe harbour," she explained. "And we've had a case of a young girl who was doing well, but after an altercation with her father, she's gone back to the streets. It's not one of our usual cases, and when I was discussing the matter with my team, someone said 'It's a shame we don't have liaison people on the street who can find them, approach them, and let them know where to get help.' The police are too busy to look for kids who aren't breaking the law or technically aren't missing. They're hiding. And I got to thinking of you, Spencer," Helen said, looking directly at me. "You found Yanni."

I blinked several times. "You want me to help find a missing kid?"

"She's fifteen and hasn't had an easy life. They're not all teens, but yes. If they're at-risk, we need to get them help."

"Mom, that's not what Spencer does," Andrew said softly.

"I'll do it." I looked at them both in turn. "If I can help one gay kid in trouble, I'll do it."

Helen beamed at me, and she squeezed my forearm. "I hoped you would. We can discuss this in more detail later. I'm sorry to talk work at this party, but I wanted to catch you before Gwendoline propositioned you."

"Mom!" Andrew hissed.

I just laughed. "She already did. I told her, very politely, I was here in the company of a man, but funnily enough that didn't deter her."

Helen laughed warmly. "She's a wicked woman. Very

brave. She helped me many years ago, and I've repaid her every year since by keeping her social calendar busy."

Someone called Mrs Landon away, and when I turned to Andrew, he was staring right back at me with a look I didn't quite recognise. "What?"

He shook his head slowly. "Do you know how remarkable you are?"

"I wasn't ever going to take Gwendoline up on her offer," I said jokingly.

He fought a smile. "You know what I mean."

"I meant what I said. If I can help one gay kid, I will."

"And that makes you remarkable."

I inhaled deeply. "I do believe my cover edition of the magazine *Remarkable and Dapper Australians* is due out next month."

He laughed at that. "Good to know."

The wait staff carried the trays out of the kitchen and Allan, Andrew's father, called for everyone's attention. "Should we go out there?" I asked Andrew.

He looked at me like I'd sprouted a second head. "Good Lord, no."

We could hear Allan as he addressed his guests with a smooth and funny and blessedly short dedication to his beautiful wife, family, and long-time friends, and of course, good food. Everyone replied with a "Cheers" or "Hear, hear," while we stayed in the kitchen. Andrew commandeered a tray of various and fancy canapés, and he no sooner shoved one into his mouth than we got sprung.

"You two! You left me out there." Sarah stalked into the grand kitchen. "We had a deal!" Then she inspected the tray Andrew was still holding before picking one. "Ooh, I love these."

Andrew laughed around his mouthful; then he turned to

me and offered the tray of food. "Mom specifically requested no shellfish when she planned the menu."

I picked up a small square of what looked like cheese, sliced peppers, and balsamic vinegar. Man, it was so good. So me, Andrew, and Sarah spent the next hour or so hiding out in the kitchen, laughing and talking crap. Eventually we made our way back out to find the small guest list even smaller. Some had a champagne flute, some had coffee, but everyone was smiling, and it was pretty obvious to me that these people had been friends for a long time. I was almost disappointed to see Gwendoline had gone home. Then again, it was about four o'clock in the afternoon; she was probably already in bed for the night. Either that or she was first in line at Avalon Hollywood all set to take body shots from some go-go boy.

I found myself talking to an older, distinguished man by the name of Davis, discussing Australian literature, of all things. He was intrigued and, dare I say it, a little impressed. But his wife soon called him away, and it wasn't long after that the only people left were us.

Allan fell into the sofa with a groan. "Promise me, my darling, we have no more 'just a few friends over for lunch' again for a while."

"Oh, it was fun." Helen laughed and collected an empty glass and handed it to the waitress. "Please bring out what canapés are left. Once I sit down, I won't be getting back up." But she walked over to the entertainment cabinet, and in the next few seconds, "Great Balls of Fire" started to play. "Oh, I love this song," she said. Helen walked over to Allan and held out her hand, a silent invitation to dance.

He waved her off. "I'm too old!"

I offered her my hand instead. "May I?"

"Oh," she swooned theatrically. "You may."

I led her to a makeshift dance floor between the furniture, and turning to face her, I took a deep breath. Then we danced, 50s-swing style. I was a little rusty, but she was very forgiving. Mr Landon laughed along with us, Andrew looked stunned but happy, and Sarah could only laugh and clap along.

By the time the song ended, we were both a little breathless. "Where did you learn how to dance like that?" Helen asked me.

"My Aunt Marvie taught me." I smiled at her. "I haven't done it in years, though, as you could probably tell."

"I haven't had a man dance with me like that in years," she said, giving her husband a mock glare.

Everyone laughed, and I knew Andrew said he didn't dance, but I figured there was no one here he would be embarrassed in front of. I walked over to where he was playing wallflower with his father on the sofa and held out my hand. "If you would do me the honour."

He was totally going to say no, but his dad and sister heckled him, and after a whole song, he finally gave in. "I can't dance," he mumbled as he begrudgingly stood up.

I led him back over to where I'd danced with his mother, and with perfect timing, the next song started. It was "Georgia On My Mind," a slow, slow song, and I pulled Andrew against me. Maybe it was weird to slow dance in front of his family, but they didn't seem to mind. When I looked over, Helen was sitting at the other end of the sofa having Allan massage her now-bare feet. "This okay?" I whispered in Andrew's ear.

"Yeah," he murmured. "Very okay."

He barely moved his feet, but it was lovely all the same. And when the next song started, he didn't pull away. I pressed my lips to his temple and spoke into his ear. "Thought you didn't like dancing?"

"Just don't want my parents to see my little problem," he mumbled, then rocked his hips into mine.

Oh. I burst out laughing. Then I whispered in his ear, "That's not a little problem."

"Oh, would you two stop it," Sarah cried. "You're making me nauseously jealous."

We broke apart with an embarrassed laugh, and Sarah shoved the tray of leftover canapés between us. "Eat. If I'm getting fat, I'm taking you both with me."

Still smiling, I picked up some round fried ball type thing and bit into it. I only took one bite, and I knew... I knew it wasn't going to end well. I tried to swallow and cough. My throat felt tight, too tight. I pulled at my top button. I tried to cough again.

Then everything kind of happened at once.

"Spencer?"

I tried to breathe. My lungs needed air, but no matter how hard I tried, I couldn't. My head throbbed, dizzy with a lack of oxygen, and I remembered thinking it was funny how it didn't hurt. And how the word anaphylaxis was really rather peculiar.

"Oh, my God, Spencer!"

"His EpiPen!" Andrew's voice was frantic. He was panicking, and I was on my back on the floor, looking up at the ceiling and their worried faces. I still couldn't breathe. "His coat. Get his coat!"

I was too hot, far too hot, and I had no air. Andrew's hands were on my face, and he was talking to me. He looked so scared. I could hear the voices. His father was close, and I felt a sharp stab in my thigh.

There was no pain. Only darkness.

EIGHT

I KNEW WHERE I WAS WITHOUT HAVING TO OPEN MY eyes. The sounds, the smell... hospital. Someone squeezed my hand, which prompted me to look.

Andrew.

He was at my side, elbows resting on my bed, my hand firmly in both of his. Our joined hands were at his face, his eyes were closed. He looked tired and like he'd aged a decade.

"Hey." My voice caught and my throat scratched, but he heard me.

His gaze shot to mine, and he visibly sagged with relief. "Oh, Spencer."

"What time...?" I couldn't even finish that sentence. "Water?"

He quickly fetched me a small cup and gently put it to my lips. The relief of the cool liquid down my throat was immediate. "Thanks."

Andrew put the cup on the table over my feet. "It's ten past eight," he said, collecting my hand again. "You've been here since five-ish. The paramedics brought you in."

I didn't remember any of it.

"Mom," Andrew called out. Almost instantly Helen, Allan, and Sarah appeared. "Can you tell them he's awake?"

"I'll go," Sarah said before disappearing.

Helen walked over to my bed. She put her hand on my arm and smiled sadly. "I'm very sorry this happened. I did specify shellfish allergy. I'll be dealing with the caterers; don't you worry."

A nurse came into the room—*Am I in a private room?*—and checked some machines and asked me how I was feeling. Then a doctor walked in, but when he discussed my "severe allergic reaction" and the drugs they'd given me, he spoke more to Andrew's parents than to me.

"When was his first allergic reaction?" the doc asked them. Did the doctor think Andrew's parents were mine as well?

Of course they wouldn't have known when I had my first allergic reaction. "When I was three," I answered. "That was the first time. And again when I was twelve."

The doctor's eyebrows furrowed. "They're getting worse, I assume?"

I nodded, then shrugged. "Maybe."

"Well, you're very lucky your step-father was there to administer the epinephrine. Or they'd be visiting you in the basement, if you know what I mean."

Basements in hospitals meant morgue. "Yeah."

"We'll keep him in overnight," the doc said. "And I suggest he not be left alone for the next 48 hours." He prattled on for a bit, but I was so tired and a bit confused.

When the doc left, Andrew took my hand and explained. "Mom told them you were her son, and Dad's your step-father," he said quietly. "They think we're brothers."

Helen patted my leg. "So he can stay in your room with you."

"Oh. Thank you." My throat scratched again, making me wince. "More water?"

Andrew stood up and helped me drink from the cup again. Then Allan said, "We'll give you two a minute." He ushered Helen and Sarah out the door.

I sighed deeply with a tiredness I could feel in my bones. Andrew put his hand to my face. "I was really fucking scared, Spencer."

I nodded. "Me too."

"You stopped breathing, and I thought you were going to die." He squeezed my hand and shook his head. He was fighting back tears. He leaned in and pressed his lips to mine. "I love you," he choked out.

Before I could reply, Lola burst into the room. She was a blur of colour and worry. She stopped dead when she saw me. "Spencer!"

Gabe followed her in, pale as a sheet. He sat down shakily. He looked up, and by way of explanation, said, "Lola drove." His eye twitched. "Faster than normal."

Lola launched herself at me, hugging what little life I had left in me. Andrew would have normally been knocked backwards, but I still had hold of his hand. I wasn't letting it go for anyone.

"You okay?" Lola asked, patting my face and hair. "Andrew phoned me. You trying to give me a heart attack?" She turned to Andrew. "Thank you. How you doing? Thank God you were there to save him."

Andrew blushed. "I'm not sure I did much. My dad was the one who stayed calm. I kinda lost my shit."

"Not true," Allan said from the doorway. "Andrew was the one who told me where the EpiPen was."

Lola put her hands to my beard and then tried to fix my hair. "Well, you scared us all by the sound of it."

Just then, a nurse came in and stopped. "Okay, who needs to be here?"

"We all do," Lola answered sweetly. Her pink hair in a fancy twist, perfect makeup, and cupcake baby-doll dress didn't fool this nurse, though.

The nurse gave a nod to me. "Mr Cohen here needs rest. Almost dying is exhausting. Visiting hours are over." Then she spotted Gabe. "Sir? Are you okay?"

Gabe looked up at her, still sweaty and pale. He waved her off. "My wife drives like Satan on acid."

I chuckled as did everyone else, and before Lola could argue, Sarah linked arms with her and they walked out. Gabe followed, Allan patted my leg, and Helen promised they'd be back first thing in the morning.

The nurse raised her eyebrow at Andrew, but he sat down beside me again. "I'm staying."

I needed to say something. He'd told me he loved me before we were interrupted, and I still hadn't said anything. But I was so tired. I just couldn't keep my eyes open any longer.

Andrew's thumb traced circles on the back of my hand before he lifted it and kissed where his thumb had just been. "Sleep, Spencer. I'll be right here."

I couldn't seem to form words, so I squeezed his hand instead and held it as tight as my tired bones would let me. And I slept.

I WOKE up when a nurse doing midnight rounds came in and checked the machine at my side. Andrew was asleep on a fold-up bed, and a warmth spread through my chest knowing he was still here.

He loved me. I knew he did. I'd heard him tell his mother before that he did. But he told *me*, he told me he loved me. It was out and couldn't be taken back. I was certain the universe had a no-take-backs clause on those three words. Not that I wanted him to take them back. God that was the last thing I wanted.

What I wanted was for my stupid brain and my even stupider heart to know what to do with those words.

The hardest part was knowing that I loved him too. My stupid brain could admit that my traitorous heart had done something I swore to myself years ago we would never do. And that was fall in love.

Yet there he slept on a fold-up bed in my hospital room. And I was in love with him. He made me the happiest man in the world. But it was those words, those three little words. I could admit to myself that I loved Andrew, I just couldn't bring myself to tell Andrew.

There was something absolutely terrifying in handing over your wounded heart for someone else to hold.

And those thoughts kept me awake, along with the constant beeps and noises that filled hospitals. Andrew woke up a little before six, confused and still half asleep, but as soon as he recognised where he was, his first thoughts were of me. "Hey. You feeling okay?" His voice croaked, and he scrubbed his hands over his face.

"Much better. Still tired but better."

He stood up and stretched the kinks out of his back. He was still wearing his clothes from yesterday, and he looked sleep-rumpled and gorgeous. He caught me staring and smiling. "What?"

"Nothing. Thank you for staying."

"I wouldn't be anywhere else."

I held my hand out to him and waited until he took it.

"I've been awake most of the night. I almost joined you on that cot."

He smiled and used my hand to scratch his stubbled jaw. "Don't think 'brothers' are supposed to be that close."

Oh, that's right. "Brothers, huh?"

"Technically step brothers, but yes."

"I would have told them it was so awfully nice of my step brother to stay the night, I just wanted to give him a cuddle in his bed."

A nurse came in and Andrew quickly dropped my hand and stood up. He went and opened the window blinds while the nurse did her routine checks and typed into the computer. "Breakfast will be around soon," she said on her way out.

Andrew made a face and quickly pulled his phone out of his pocket. He texted something, then looked at me. "You're not eating hospital food."

"I'm actually kinda hungry."

"So am I, but hospital food is what they serve in gastronomical hell."

I chuckled, which woke up my bladder. "I need to piss."

"Oh, let me help you," Andrew said, putting his hand on my shoulder.

"You wanna hold it for me?"

He laughed. "Don't think they'll appreciate that."

"I'm fine," I assured him, getting to my feet and manoeuvring my IV pole with me. "I can get up."

He bit his lip.

"Not that," I said with a snort. "Well, I can get that up too, but I'd rather not have a piss-on when the doctor comes in."

"A piss-on?"

"Like a hard-on, but just morning and a full bladder, you know how it is?" I walked over to the private bathroom door, wheeling my saline drip with me. "Can you see my arse through this gown?"

"Ah, yes."

I wiggled my arse. "Good." I closed the door behind me, relieved my bladder, then washed my hands and my face. Hospitals always made me feel dirty. I stood with my back to the door so Andrew would have a perfect view of my arse and reaching behind me, I opened the door. "You know, these gowns could come in handy. We should see if I can take this home."

Only Andrew didn't laugh. Sarah did. Really loudly. I spun around. Andrew slowly put his hands over his face, Sarah was now bent over silent-laughing, Andrew's parents, who were holding drinks and food, were both trying *not* to laugh, and the doctor rose one eyebrow and nodded slowly before saying, "I think you can keep it."

I'm pretty sure I was bright red from my head to my feet. My voice squeaked, "I didn't know... God, I'm really sorry."

"I take it you're feeling better?" the doctor asked.

"Much." Still not making eye contact with anyone in the room, I walked around them and sat on the bed, making sure everything was duly covered. "Can I go home, please? I'd much rather die of embarrassment there."

A nurse breezed in, removed my IV line without so much as a word, and when she was done, the doc's expression went from amused to serious. He gave me a lecture about severe allergies, like I didn't know, and he gave me the nod to be discharged. "Like I said last night, I'd prefer you weren't left alone for 48 hours. And you need to come back at the first sign of dizziness or nausea, shortness of breath, swelling."

"I can stay with him," Andrew said.

The doc smirked. "A nurse will be around with the paper-work. Just don't let her catch you stealing the gown."

"I was joking about that. I'm really very sorry," I mumbled as fresh waves of embarrassment rolled through me.

The doctor left, and Andrew was the first to laugh. He clapped his hands together and rocked up on his toes. "Well, now that everyone's seen your backside." I threw the pillow at him. It was like a brick. I hoped it hurt, but he caught it easily.

"Here you go, my dear," Helen said, handing me a white takeout cup. "Green tea. Andrew told me what to order. And there's pastries as well."

Allan held out the bag he was holding. "No shellfish. I asked."

I smiled as I took a sip of my tea. It was heavenly. "Thank you. Thank you all, for everything. For the tea, for saving my life yesterday, for pretending I didn't show you my backside. And for telling them we were related so Andrew could stay."

Helen smiled. "Ah yes, it's not exactly lying when it's acting. And I can still give quite the credible performance. No one questioned me."

"Well, thank you. I appreciate it."

"After yesterday, it's the least we could do," Allan said.

"I don't blame anyone," I told them. "These things happen." No one looked convinced at all. So I sipped my tea again and released a sigh. "This is great tea. Thank you."

Andrew sat on the bed, took a long drink of his coffee, and looked into the bag of pastries. He pulled out one and handed it to me. Then he picked one and bit into it. "Mmm, so much better than hospital food."

"Oh," Sarah said. "Lola wants you to call her first thing."

I looked at Sarah. "Can you please hand me my phone? I don't even know where it is."

There was a bag that was on Andrew's fold-up bed next to my pile of clothes. I assumed it had my belongings in it but wasn't sure. Andrew pointed to it and mumbled something with a mouthful of food. His mother chided him, and he rolled his eyes. Such a normal family. Incredibly wonderful and loving but perfectly normal.

Sarah passed me my phone and wallet, and when I checked the phone, the battery was dead. "Oh boy, she won't be happy with me."

Andrew held up his phone and mumbled something with a mouthful of food. Sarah rolled her eyes at him. "You're so gross." Then she said to me, "I'm sure I still have her number. When we'd made plans to meet you that first time, remember?" She quickly had her phone out and was thumbing through pages. "Yep, here it is. Want me to call her?"

"If you could, please just text her and tell her I'll be home in..." I looked at Andrew. "I don't even know what hospital I'm in."

He rubbed my leg and thankfully had swallowed his food. "Tell Lola he'll be home within the hour."

"Thank you," I said, leaning back on the bed.

"You look tired," he said softly.

"I didn't sleep much last night."

"How about you get dressed, and as soon as the paperwork's done, I'll take you home."

I nodded. "Sounds great." Then I remembered something. "Hey, isn't it Monday? Shouldn't you be going to work?"

"I can take some leave. I have plenty."

As much as I didn't want him to miss work on my behalf, the idea of spending the day in bed with him was too good to pass up. I finished my pastry, some Danish type thing, and walked to the bathroom. Grateful to be unhooked from the IV line and holding the back of my robe, of course.

I grabbed a quick shower and dressed in the clothes I wore yesterday. I was feeling a little better when I walked back out. A nurse was waiting, none-too patiently, for me to fill out paperwork. I read through the forms, and the nurse made some comment about young people being inadequately insured, to which I replied, "Australian and American medical and hospital insurances are so very different, and getting proper insurance was one of the first things I did when I got here. I'd heard horror stories of people paying crazy amounts of money for emergency care because they weren't insured. I figured, knowing my luck, I'd have a reaction and die in a waiting room." I signed and handed the clipboard back to the nurse.

She looked over the paperwork. "You don't have a next of kin listed."

I put the pen down. It took me a little while to answer. "No."

I could feel everyone's eyes on me, but it was Andrew who cleared his throat and took a protective step closer to me. "Okay, we can go now?" He put his hand on the small of my back. "You ready?"

I nodded. "Yeah."

Thankfully, Allan had driven Andrew's car to the hospital, as he'd left it at his parents' house when I'd suddenly decided to try and die yesterday. With more goodbyes and twenty more thank yous to his family, Andrew and I both got hugs before we were allowed to leave.

I slid into the passenger seat, feeling every hour of sleep I'd missed. Andrew put his hand on my knee. "You need to sleep."

I couldn't even argue. I let my head fall onto the headrest and closed my eyes. "Mmhmm. Wanna join me?"

"To sleep, yes," he said, navigating out of the car park. "I'm pretty sure the doctor said no physical exertion for two days."

I didn't open my eyes. "That's okay. I'll just lie there. You can do all the work."

He chuckled but he didn't agree. He was quiet for the rest of the drive back to my place, in what I assumed was an attempt to let me rest. When we parked at the back of the shop, I trudged up the stairs and Andrew opened my door. I knew Lola and probably everyone else would be coming up at some point, and I had no idea if Andrew needed to go anywhere, but I kicked off my shoes and pulled off my shirt, then walked over to my kitchen drawer. I pulled out my spare key and walked sleepily over to Andrew.

I still hadn't acknowledged the fact he'd told me he loved me. I wasn't sure I could. So instead I held out my hand. "I want you to have this."

Andrew's gaze shot to mine.

"If you need to leave and come back," I told him. "And if I'm still asleep."

"Oh." He couldn't hide the hurt on his face.

I grabbed his shirt to keep him right where he was. "No. Not just that. I know what it means, and I know it's a huge step. It's more than a toothbrush, and I'm okay with that. I'm giving you a key to my place so you can come by any time. You don't need to ask. I will never say no." I slow-blinked. "I want you to have it."

"Spencer," he whispered. "Thank you."

I leaned in and kissed him. "You're welcome."

"God, you can hardly keep your eyes open," he mumbled, taking my hand and leading me to my room. "Into bed with you."

I undid my pants and pulled them down, getting into bed wearing just my boxer briefs. Andrew pulled the blankets up over me then picked up my pants. He put my wallet on the bedside table and put my phone on charge, like he was trying to distract himself and keep himself busy.

"Thank you," I said, sounding tired to my own ears. I patted the bed. "Sit for a sec."

He hesitated but did as I asked. "What's up?"

"Are you okay?"

"Sure. Why wouldn't I be?"

"It um, couldn't have been too pleasant to watch me have that allergic reaction."

He let out a laugh that didn't sound too happy. "You almost died, Spencer. You stopped breathing. And no one explained to me that once we injected an EpiPen into you, that you'd shake like that."

I groaned. "I'm sorry. It must have been horrible."

"It was," Andrew replied quietly. He looked right at me. "But it wasn't your fault, so don't apologise."

"I'm still sorry. I wish you didn't have to see that. The shaking is a side-effect, or so I'm told. Not everyone does that. I didn't know I did, sorry."

He nodded and gave me a sad smile; his eyes shone with tears. "I was so scared."

I grabbed his hand. "Hey. Lie down here." I pulled him down and close so he was the little spoon and wrapped my arm around him. "I'm here."

He relaxed into me and pulled my arm tighter around him. Just when I couldn't fight sleep a second longer, I heard him whisper, "I'm here too."

I WOKE up to the sound of Janis Joplin singing about me and Bobby McGee. The curtains were drawn in my room so I had no idea what time it was, but I was alone. I heard voices—

Andrew, Emilio, and Lola—coming from the lounge room, so I rolled out of bed, pulled on some shorts, grabbed my phone, and went out there.

"Hey, here he is," Emilio said, standing up to greet me. "How you feeling, man?"

"Still a bit tired. What time is it?" I asked, as I checked my phone. It was lunch time. No wonder I was hungry.

Lola hugged me and patted me all over. "You okay? Need me to grab you something."

"I feel okay. Hungry, but if you could hold the shellfish, that'd be great." There was a beat of silence. "What? Too soon?"

Andrew smirked. "Not funny."

I fell into the lounge next to Andrew and slid against him, leaning on his chest. I pulled his arm over my shoulder and sighed. "It was kinda funny."

Lola was in the kitchen. "Want a sandwich, Spence?"

"I would love one."

"I'll help," I said, trying to get up.

"No, I will," Andrew said, shuffling me off him and standing up.

"You'll help?" I asked. "Cooking?"

He turned back to face me. "Making sandwiches isn't cooking, smartass."

Emilio laughed, which made me look at him. "Not busy today?"

"Got a client at two. Thought I'd come up and see how you were getting on. Andrew said you weren't in real good shape last night."

I sighed. "Yeah. It wasn't good. I was lucky he was there, and his parents."

"You got more of those EpiPens?"

"Yeah, of course."

"I still got the one in the reception drawer," he said. "I checked after Lola told us. She has one in her car, in her bag. You give Andrew some for his place?"

"I will."

He put on his I'm-being-serious face. "I mean it."

His protectiveness was a sure sign of how much he cared. I gave him a smile. "I know. And thanks."

I turned my phone on and got a buzzing reward of a dozen messages and missed calls.

"Come get it," Lola called out from the kitchen.

I hauled my tired arse off the sofa and stood up as I began to scroll through the missed calls, when one in particular caught my eye. It wasn't just one call, it was three. The international dial code was 612...

Australia.

"Spencer, what is it?" Andrew stood in front of me, holding a plate with a sandwich on it. I hadn't realised I'd stopped walking.

I blinked a few times and cleared my throat. "I have some missed calls from home. I mean, Australia."

Andrew looked to my phone, then back to my eyes. "Is there a message?"

I thumbed to my voicemail. By this time, Emilio and Lola were standing, watching me. I hit the message and put it on speaker. "Hello Spencer. This is Terrence Ascot from Barkley Solomons. Please call me back at this number."

My heart was beating erratically against my ribs. "Well, this can't be good," I mumbled. I checked my watch. Just after one in the afternoon here meant just after eight in the morning over there. I cleared my throat so I could somehow manage to speak. "Terrence is my solicitor."

Knowing Terrence worked early till late, I hit Call. After a few rings, a woman answered. "Good morning, Barkley Solomons, Terrence Ascot's office."

I took a deep breath and looked right at Andrew when I said, "Spencer Cohen, returning Terrence Ascot's call."

She put me on hold to transfer the call, but when he answered, I clicked off speaker and put the phone to my ear. I didn't want everyone to hear this. I would tell them, of course, but only after I'd processed the information.

"Sorry I missed your calls," I said. "I had a bit of an emergency yesterday."

"Everything okay?"

Oh, sure. Just nearly died. Nothing major. "Yes, everything's fine."

There was a beat of silence before I heard him take a deep breath like he was steeling himself to give bad news. I knew then it wasn't good. Solicitors didn't struggle for words unless the news they were to deliver was difficult to say.

I figured I'd save him the trouble. "Last time we spoke it was to inform me of the death of my Aunt. Don't suppose you charge more to tell me good news?"

There was a quiet sigh. "Unfortunately, Spencer, this is not good news either. I've been contacted by a Mr Lewis Cohen."

"Oh." Lewis was my brother. This was not what I expected. I didn't know what I'd expected, but that God-awful hope ballooned in my chest without my permission.

"Yes," my lawyer said. "He asked me to forward on some rather unpleasant news."

I waited.

"Archer Cohen, your youngest brother, passed away."

The expanded balloon in my chest burst, taking the air from my lungs with it. I unsteadily sat on my sofa, and Andrew sat beside me. He took my hand and tethered me to that moment. That simple touch, a tangible lifeline, when I felt like drowning. "What?"

"He took his own life. I'm very sorry to be the one to tell you. Lewis contacted my office, unbeknownst to your father. He asked, if you're agreeable, that I forward his contact details on to you. He wishes to speak with you. I can email the information to you if you'd prefer."

"Yes," I whispered in return. I wasn't capable of doing anything more. My head was foggy, and my vision started to blur.

"Spencer," he continued softly, "for what it's worth, he was very genuine. His reply when I asked him why I should cause you any more grief than necessary was, and I quote, 'Spencer is all the family I have left.'"

I didn't hear what he said after that.

Andrew took the phone from me and slid it onto the side table. He took both my hands in his. "Spencer, what is it?"

I don't know how I even spoke. "My brother died... He committed suicide."

No one said a word, except Bill Withers started to sing "Ain't No Sunshine." Lola walked over to the record player and quietly lifted the tonearm, and Andrew squeezed my hand.

I went kinda numb after that.

NINE

I SPENT THE NEXT HOWEVER LONG CURLED UP IN MY papasan chair, staring into space. Emilio, Lola, and Andrew were whispering in the kitchen, and I couldn't bring myself to listen or care.

After a while, Emilio came over and put his hand on my shoulder. "I'll be back up later. Okay, my friend? If you need anything, I'm just downstairs, okay?"

I managed to nod.

Then Lola kissed the top of my head and hugged me. "I'll be back in a little while too, 'kay Spence? I just need to go make some arrangements for tomorrow. I'll bring some dinner back with me, okay?"

The haze in my mind shifted. "What's happening tomorrow?"

Lola looked so damn sad. "I have a four hour photoshoot tomorrow. I'll see if I can get Angelica to cover it for me."

I wasn't following. "Why?"

"So I can be here with you."

I shook my head. "No, it's fine, Lola. I'll be fine. Just stop by afterwards."

"Honey, it's no big deal. I want to be here with you."

"Thank you, but honestly, I'll be fine. I am fine. And Emilio," I said, finally looking at him. "No need to come check on me. I'll come down later, I just need some time, if that's okay?"

Lola and Emilio looked at each other, then at Andrew, then at me. "You sure?"

I cleared my throat. "Yeah. I appreciate it, though. More than you know. I just need some space to get my thoughts in order, ya know?"

They both nodded silently, and Lola lightly touched Andrew's arm as they walked out. I'd probably need to apologise to them both tomorrow, but for now, I really just needed silence.

I got up and went into the kitchen. The sandwich they'd made for me sat untouched on the counter. I considered eating it, but when I went to pick it up, my stomach rolled.

"You okay?" Andrew asked gently.

I nodded again, still staring at the chicken and mayo sandwich. "I feel like a Vegemite sandwich," I whispered. "I haven't had one since we were kids."

Andrew put his hand on my back. "Did you want to talk about him?"

I shook my head. "Not right now."

He dropped his hand. "Okay."

When I looked at him, he was biting his lip. He looked worried and sad. "What's wrong?"

"I'm worried about you."

"I'm okay." But that wasn't it. He wouldn't hold eye contact. "What's really wrong?"

"Did you want me to go?"

What? "No."

"You said you needed time and space, and if you don't

want Emilio or Lola here, then I can only assume you certainly don't want me here either. You can tell me, you know. I'll understand."

I shook my head. "I don't want you to go." Jesus, it was the last thing I wanted.

"What do you need?" he asked me softly.

I sighed and pushed the sandwich away. "Not that."

He nodded slowly. "Okay. Are you hungry?"

"No."

He looked stung and lost for what to say.

"Sorry," I whispered. I hung my head and took a deep breath. He stayed where he was, a very obvious distance between us. "I don't know what I need right now."

"Lola and Emilio just want to help you," he said softly. "Don't push them away."

"I know that." I turned to face him then, and he looked about ready to leave.

He nodded, and I swear he took a small step backwards. "Okay."

"Why are you leaving?"

"I'm not."

"Then what's wrong?"

He shook his head. "Nothing."

"Andrew, please. I don't have the energy for games right now. If there's something wrong, please just tell me."

"I'm trying not to say the wrong things," he whispered to the ground between us. "I always say the wrong things, especially at the wrong time. I tend to ruin things, even the best things. Like before..."

"Like before, when?"

"In the hospital." He quickly shook his head. "Look, this isn't the time for this conversation. Because this is not about me. You've had the worst two days, and you're dealing with so much right now, I can't even imagine."

In the hospital. He told me he loved me, and I haven't mentioned it.

"Now's the very right time. Considering everything—me almost dying, my brother..." I swallowed down the lump in my throat. "Considering that, now is the best time."

"I'm waiting for you to push me away."

"What?"

"I figured what I told you in the hospital... and now the news of your brother. I don't know. I'm waiting for you to feel too overwhelmed." He shrugged. "But me telling you that I love you is true. I do. I won't apologise for saying it. And maybe now is the very time you need to hear it."

I closed my eyes and nodded.

Andrew's voice cracked when he continued, "I tried not to expect you to say it back to me, but I guess I did, and that's not fair on you. Especially now. "

I tried to calm my hammering heart. "No."

Andrew frowned. "Oh."

I could barely speak. "No." He tried to take a step backwards but my hand was fisted in his shirt. "No. Wait. Please."

He lifted my face so I looked at him. "Spencer, I don't know what you need."

"Andrew, I need you. That's all. Yes, I need time and I need space but *not* from you. I need you to be here with me. I don't know how I'm supposed to deal with anything right now, but I can't do any of it without you." I took a shaky breath. "I can't... I can't say *that*. What you want me to say. I wish I could. But I'm not ready." Andrew tried to pull away, but I still had hold of his shirt. "Just because I can't say it doesn't mean it's not true. Because what you said to me in the hospital," I whispered, "means everything."

Andrew took my face in his hands. "You mean that?"

I barely nodded. My voice cracked when I said, "Please don't leave me."

He kissed me so tenderly, then held me so tight. I wanted to crawl inside him, I wanted him to never let me go. He held me in such a way that I could feel him healing the hurt inside me. I was so confused, lost and heartbroken. He kissed the side of my head. "I'm not going anywhere."

For the longest time, neither of us spoke. We just stood there, holding and deep breathing, and soul-mending. With a deep breath, I mumbled into his neck, "My solicitor said Lewis contacted him and asked him to get in touch with me. He said I was the only family he had left."

Andrew pulled back and put his hand to my face. "Does he want to talk with you?"

"I don't know. I think so. My solicitor was going to email me his contact details."

He spoke like I was made from glass. "That's a good thing, isn't it?"

I blinked back tears, like I'd been torn wide open. "What if... what if he just shuts me out again? What if he decides that our father was right and that he regrets speaking to me? Andrew, I can't go through that again."

Andrew put both hands to my face and ran his thumbs over my cheeks, as though I was the most precious thing in his world. "I'll talk to him first. I'll see what he has to say; then you can decide if you speak to him, not the other way around. If you want, that is."

I nodded. "I want to speak to him. But I'm scared."

Andrew pulled me back against him, one arm around my back, one hand in my hair. "I'll be with you."

"Thank you."

He led me back to the sofa, where he proceeded to lie

down and pull me with him so I was the little spoon. I felt safe and loved and utterly exhausted. He kissed the back of my head, and I closed my eyes, somehow falling asleep.

I dreamed of an Australian summer and a holiday at the beach. But the sky became clouded and the wind turned cold. I was running on the beach and a sixteen year old me searched for a twelve year old Archie, and no matter how hard I looked, no matter how much I called and screamed his name, he was lost.

ANDREW WAS MY SAFETY NET. He never said anything when I stared into space; he never questioned me when I woke up frantic and upset. He was just there, so I knew I wasn't alone—so I *wasn't* alone. With a gentle touch when I craved it, a reassuring smile when I needed it, he was ever-present without being overbearing. He was my two feet on solid ground when I felt like I was in quicksand.

He took the phone number my solicitor had given me and made the call to Lewis. I sat in my papasan chair with my knees drawn up, wishing I was strong enough to make this call myself.

But the truth was, I wasn't.

"Hello, is this Lewis Cohen? ... My name is Andrew Landon, I'm calling from America. Do you have a moment to talk? ... I'm Spencer's boyfriend. ... Yes, that's right. He spoke to his solicitor this morning."

I couldn't hear what Lewis was saying, and I chewed my thumbnail half wishing I could hear every word, half glad I couldn't.

"You have to understand why he's hesitant. ... Yes, I guess I am. I wanted to see if you were genuine. ... Yes, I know. ...

Okay, I'll check with him. Give me one sec. ... No, he's right here." Andrew put the phone against his chest and gave me a sad, sad smile. "He wants to talk to you. Is that okay?"

"Is he...?"

Andrew's voice was a whisper. "He's crying. I think you should talk to him."

Oh God. I took the phone and swallowed down the lump in my throat. "Lewis?"

My brother's voice was just as I remembered, like I hadn't been gone a day. "Spencer?" He sobbed into the phone. "My God, I've missed you so much."

I burst into tears, and Andrew held my hand.

I SPOKE to Lewis for about an hour. Our conversation ranged from Archie's funeral two days ago to the time the three of us rode our bikes to Bronte Beach and nine-year-old Archie couldn't ride back up the hill. Man, we got our arses kicked for thinking he could keep up with us. And that time when I was fourteen, Lewis and I made Archie watch Stephen King's *It* the night before we were supposed to be going to the circus.

Yeah, we got in trouble for that too.

I told Lewis about the time a three-year-old Archie pulled the tape out of all the cassettes I'd gotten for my seventh birthday. I'd bugged our mother to the point of breaking for the Backstreet Boys, and Archie pulled its insides out with his Vegemite covered hands the day after I got it. Lewis laughed and laughed. "I'd forgotten that!" Then he sighed. "He still ate Vegemite sandwiches." I could tell he was fighting tears again. "Fuck, Spencer. Everything's such a mess."

"I know."

"I never saw it coming. I never thought for one minute

he'd do himself in. I swear it. I talked to him just the day before, and he seemed okay." He was crying again. "He left a note, Spencer. Fucking hell."

"What did it say?"

"Oh man, I…" He sobbed. "I can't…"

I nodded, even though he couldn't see. "Was it about me?"

"No. Not directly." It sounded like he shook his head and ground out a frustrated sound. "I'm so sick of crying. Spencer, can I see you? I know it's a lot to ask, but I need to see you."

"You want me to come to Australia?" I asked Lewis, and Andrew's gaze shot to mine.

"Just to visit, if you can," Lewis answered quickly. It sounded like he rubbed his free hand over his face. "I don't think I can leave Mum and Dad right now, even though…"

"Even though, what?"

"Even though I don't want to be here. Spencer, I won't tell them you're here. They won't know. I'll pay for your ticket."

"I'll think about it," I told him. "I just, I just never thought I'd go back there, Lewy. I don't know if I can."

He sniffed into the phone. "Yeah. I get that. I'm sorry for asking. But I would really like to see you. Maybe in a couple of months I could fly over there? It's just that…"

There was something he wasn't telling me.

"What is it Lewis? What won't you tell me?"

"I hate them," he spat out angrily. "I fucking hate them. They tore our family apart. They kicked you out and drove Archie to the point where he couldn't see any way out." He was crying again, a mix of anger and frustration. "They've taken everything away from me."

"Well, I'm back now," I offered lamely. "We're talking, huh?"

"Yeah. Think it over. Please."

"Okay."

"Can I call you? In a day or something?"

"Of course. Whenever you need."

We said our goodbyes and ended the call. I threw my phone onto the coffee table, leaned back in the sofa, and sighed.

Andrew was sitting beside me again. "You okay?"

I looked at him. "I am." I smiled wearily. "I actually feel better."

"He wants you to go to Sydney?"

I nodded. "He wants to see me. He's a bit of a mess."

"That's understandable."

"Yeah. It is."

"It's good though, right? Talking to him?"

I nodded again and gave him the best smile I could manage. "Thank you for being here."

"I wouldn't be anywhere else. Doctor's orders, remember? He said you needed supervision for the next two days. I'm making it my civic duty."

"I'm civically grateful."

Andrew smiled. "You hungry?"

"I am, actually."

He handed me his phone. "Lola called me. While you were talking to Lewis. I didn't want to interrupt. She and Gabe are coming over, but can you call her? She's very worried. And so is Emilio. He's downstairs pacing."

"Is he really?"

"Well, okay, maybe not pacing, but you're his best friend, Spencer. Let them help you. They love you and they need to help you right now. Don't let them think you don't need them, because they need you."

I nodded slowly. "Okay, I get it. I'll go see him."

Andrew grinned and stood. He held out his hand. "Come

on. I'm going to grab some dinner for all of us while you talk to Emilio. Lola'll be there soon."

He started to walk to the door but I pulled him back. "Stop." I slid my arm around him and pressed my forehead to his. "Thank you. Andrew, you have no idea how grateful I am for you."

He put his hand on my cheek and kissed me. "And I am grateful for you."

WHEN I WALKED into Emilio's shop, he was standing next to the curtained cubicles, talking with Daniela. As soon as they saw me, their conversation stopped, and Emilio strode over and hugged me.

"Thank you," I whispered before he let me go.

"No problem." He pulled back and clapped my shoulder. "How are you doing?"

"Better."

Andrew spoke then. "I'm just gonna go grab a few things for dinner. We'll eat here, right?"

Daniela nodded and put her hand on his arm. "We would like that, very much."

We watched him leave, and Emilio said, "He's a good man."

I blew a breath out through puffed out cheeks. "He really is."

"You look exhausted. Come, sit down," Emilio insisted.

I all but fell into the sofa in his waiting room, and Emilio and Daniela joined me. "I spoke to my brother, Lewis."

"And how was that?" Emilio asked. "How was he?"

"He's not doing so great. But I think we cleared the air between us."

Daniela smiled warmly. "Oh, Spencer, that's wonderful."

I nodded and let out a long breath. "Yeah it is. He wants to see me. Well, he wants me to fly to Sydney."

Emilio frowned. "Will you?"

"I don't know. I just don't know."

Lola and Gabe arrived then, and Lola hugged me and I held her just as fiercely. She was tiny, but by God, she was strong, then Gabe hugged me too. So I recounted my conversation with Lewis for her as well, and by the time I'd recounted Andrew's gentle lecture about me not pushing my friends away, he came through the front door of the tattoo shop with a carton of beer under one arm and a grocery bag in his other hand.

"Jesus," Gabe muttered, jumping off the chair to help him.

"Wasn't so bad," Andrew said as Gabe relieved him of the carton of beer.

"He can carry twice that," I said with a smile. "He's ripped as hell under that sweater vest."

Andrew jokingly narrowed his eyes at me. "Because I go to the gym while your lazy ass is still in bed."

I shrugged. "True."

Then Andrew said, "I had to go into that import grocery store two blocks over to get dinner." He held up the grocery bag. It didn't look like it would feed six people... He reached into the bag and pulled out a jar of Vegemite. "Vegemite sandwiches"—he looked right at me—"in honour of Archie. I heard Lewis say they were still his favourite."

I refused to cry, but I stood up and walked over to him and hugged him so fucking hard he squeaked. "You're squashing the bread."

I pulled back and kissed him softly. "Thank you."

"Anytime. Anything." He breathed in deep. "And if this

Vegemite tastes like crap to us all non-Australians, we can order Chinese food."

Emilio shut the shop for the night, and we sat around his waiting room eating Vegemite sandwiches and drinking beer. They hated every bite but choked them down anyway. I savoured every mouthful; the taste of my childhood brought with it fresh memories. We talked, we laughed, and I recalled a story or two of me and my brothers from when we were kids.

And as I looked at my friends, sitting with me, sharing my grief, and helping me heal, I thought, this is what family is. This right here. It didn't get any better than this.

And the next morning, I lay in bed thinking, and when Andrew woke, he found me staring at the ceiling. He asked, "You okay?"

I turned my head and gave him a smile. "Yeah. Andrew, I wanna go back to Sydney."

TEN

"Wʜᴀᴛ?"

"I want to see Lewis."

He blinked and scrubbed his hands over his face. "Okay."

After I'd let him wake up a bit, I said, "I want to go today. Or tomorrow. I don't want to put it off any longer. It's been years since I've seen him. And last night got me thinking: I have this here. I have a family in my friends here. Emilio and Lola are the best brother and sister I could ever ask for. And you... well, you're not a brother because that'd be weird considering what we did last night. But Lewis has no one. He said he's alone. He's detached from my parents; he lost his closest brother. Andrew, he was so upset..."

Andrew patted my chest then rolled over and sat up on the edge of the bed. "I'll make some phone calls."

I was a little confused, but he went to the bathroom and came back to the bedroom. He sat on the bed, leaning against the headboard, phone in his hand. "How many days will we be gone?"

We? "Um." I sat up and scratched my head. "We?"

He looked from his phone to me. "Well, I just assumed... Do you not want me to come with you?"

"I don't know. I hadn't given it any thought," I said with a shake of my head. "But yes. If you can, that is."

"Well, I have a lot of vacation time accrued at work. So that won't be a problem." He frowned. "Is this moving too fast? Is going away together this early in our relationship a good idea?"

"I have no clue."

"I just don't want you to go through that alone." He held out his hand, and I took it without hesitation. "Are you sure it's okay if I go along?"

"Yes. Of course, yes. I would like that very much." I squeezed his hand. "I don't care if it's too soon in our relationship. I know this trip won't be easy; there will be memories and demons and..." I inhaled deeply. "I would appreciate it very much if you were with me."

He looked at me for a long moment, like he found me to be peaceful to look at. Then he went back to thumbing through his phone, and when he found what he was looking for, he showed me the screen. "There's a flight tonight at ten? I guess that's so we arrive at a half-decent time."

I booked two tickets, and Andrew left to make arrangements and get organised and packed. He promised to see me back at my place as soon as he was done, and with a lingering kiss at my front door, he left.

I shot an email to Lewis giving him flight numbers; then I went downstairs and told Emilio. He was shocked. That much was clear. Without taking his eyes off me, he put down the papers he was holding. "You're coming back, right?"

"Of course!"

He exhaled loudly. "Okay then. Good." He smiled, relieved. "You told Lola yet?"

I pulled out my phone. "Not yet. Wish me luck." Emilio chuckled and went back to his papers while I waited for Lola to answer.

"Hey, Spence," she answered warmly. "How you doing this morning?"

"I'm surprisingly okay. What are you doing this evening, around eight?"

"Um, nothing. Why?"

"Well, I was hoping you could drive us to LAX?"

"Why? Why would... where are you going? Are you going to Australia? Spencer, please tell me you intend to come back."

"Yes. Of course I am. Emilio wondered the same thing."

"Well, of course we would. And Andrew didn't?" she asked. "Oh please tell me you've told him you're going. And for the love of Jeff Buckley, please tell me you told him you were coming home? Spencer?"

"I'm coming back! And of course I told Andrew. He's coming with me!"

"Oh," she said with a relieved sigh.

"I was kinda hoping you could drive us?"

"Sure I can. Is he ready to meet Cindy Crawford?"

"Well, I figured if he's brave enough to endure a trip in Cindy Crawford, then we can survive going away together."

There was a beat of silence. "Spencer Cohen, don't think for one second that Australian accent works on me. I am deeply offended."

I smiled when I answered, "You're the *best* best friend I could ever ask for."

"I'll be there for dinner. Just in case you didn't follow, you're buying." She sniffed. "And I love you too." The phone went dead in my ear.

I slid my phone into my pocket, and somehow, I lost track

of time. I got busy helping Emilio, then Daniela. I ran some errands, made some calls, and after I'd ordered pizza to be delivered for dinner, I took a phone call from Helen Landon. Firstly, she wanted me to know how very sorry she was to hear the news of my brother and wanted to know if there was anything at all she could do. After I had told her I was okay, she wanted to give me a lecture—gently, but still a lecture—about taking her son overseas and taking proper care of him, then she lectured me about taking care of myself because the last time she saw me, I was in hospital. Lastly, she asked me if I was still interested in helping her at the Acacia Foundation, finding at-risk LGBTIQ people.

She had mentioned one girl in particular, and I would assume each case was time sensitive. "I'll be away almost a week," I explained. "We have return tickets for five days. I'm not sure if I'm any help right now. Otherwise I would love to. It's something that would mean a great deal to me."

"The offer stands for when you get back. We can discuss details then."

Daniela answered a knock at the back door, and Andrew walked back in with her. "He's talking to your mom," Daniela said to him.

Andrew stared and then held out his hand for my phone. I grimaced. "Uh, Andrew's here. He wants to talk to you."

He took the phone and put it to his ear. "Mom. I said not to call him!" He listened and mumbled a few responses while me, Emilio, and Daniela looked on, trying not to smile. When he was done, he ended the call and gave me back my phone. "I'm sorry."

I kissed his cheek. "It was a nice surprise."

He sighed. "You ready? I've been to work. Got approved vacation time for eight days. I figured a few days off when we get back can't hurt. I don't do jet lag very well. I organised with Sarah to check on my place. She's coming here to pick up my keys; I told her it'd be okay if I left them here?" he looked at Emilio. Emilio nodded, and Andrew kept on talking. "I'm packed and ready, passport, I had to google what the weather was like in Sydney this time of year... Why are you looking at me?"

I checked my watch. "Oh. I kinda lost track of time."

He stared.

"I organised Lola to drive us to the airport. That counts, right?"

He looked at me like I'd just spoken in tongues.

"I'm taking that's a no."

"I'm trying really hard not to say something awkward or offensive. You know I struggle with saying the wrong thing." He looked at Emilio and Daniela. "I tend to ruin things by saying the wrong thing, and it's something I'm working on. Like now." He looked back at me and ran his hand through his hair. He let out a long breath. "We're leaving here in just over an hour, Spencer, to fly half way around the world. I know it's not under the best circumstances, and I'm trying to be understanding, but I'm stressing out because I've never left the country with half a day notice before."

I put my fingers to his lips to cut him off. "I ordered pizza. Should be here in ten."

"Spencer."

I gave him my best smile. "Don't stress. She'll be right."

He narrowed his eyes. "Your *Australian* won't work on me."

I chuckled. "Lola said the same thing."

"She'll be right?" he repeated. "Who is she?"

"No one. It's just something Aussie's say. As in everything'll be fine."

He mumbled something that sounded like needing a

lobotomy, and he let out a long suffering sigh. "What kind of pizza did you order?"

He really was too easy. Pizza arrived, as did Lola, and we spent an hour or so talking about our trip. Andrew stood up, his patience worn thin, and packed up the empty boxes. "I'll take these out," he said, disappearing through the back.

"He's nervous," I whispered to the others. "I didn't expect him to come with me, but I'm so glad he is."

"Take him upstairs," Lola said. "Finish getting ready, and I'll be up in ten to get you."

I smiled at her. "Thanks. I um, I haven't packed anything yet. So if you hear him yelling…"

"Oh, Spencer," Lola said.

"'Oh, Spencer' what?" Andrew said, walking back in.

"Nothing," I answered, quickly getting up and walking over to him. "Come on. Better get organised."

His whole demeanour changed from impatient to excited. He took the stairs two at a time and waited for me at the top, but I took the stairs slower than him, marvelling in the beauty of his arse. "Didn't I give you a key?" I asked him.

"Yes." He looked at the door then back down to me. "I can't use my key to your place when you're with me. That'd be weird."

I got to the top landing. "I'd like you to use your key."

"Will it make you get ready sooner?"

"Yes."

He fished his keys from his pocket, found the one I'd given him, and simply opened the door. "Happy now?"

I gave him a smiley sigh. "Another first to go on my 'Because of Andrew' list."

Andrew recoiled, he looked at the door, then to me, then to the keys in his hand, and his face fell. "Sorry. I should have realised. I didn't mean to be so insensitive."

As I walked past him, I planted a kiss on his lips. "You are completely and utterly forgiven. You're giving up a lot to come with me."

Andrew closed the door behind us. "I'm not giving up anything. I want to go with you."

I emptied my pockets onto the kitchen counter. "Your boss didn't mind?"

Andrew shook his head. "Nah. Was surprised, but when I told him what we were going for, he said it was fine. I have a tonne of vacation time accrued. Shell was kinda pissed that I was leaving her for a week. It meant that she has to suffer through lunch breaks with Antonio from Production. I told her I'll buy her a stuffed toy kangaroo to make up for it."

I walked into my room, pulled my suitcase out from the back of the wardrobe, and threw it on the bed. "And you're completely okay with travelling overseas for a week with your boyfriend of two months?"

Andrew smiled, but his patience was clearly worn a little thin. "I am. I don't want you to go through that alone."

"I'd come back, you know," I told him. Both Lola and Emilio had initially thought I would stay, and I had to wonder if Andrew thought the same.

His gaze shot to mine. "What?"

"I'd come back. If I were to go to Sydney by myself, I would come back to LA. This is my home now. If that's what you're worried about."

Andrew sighed but somehow managed to smile. "I know that. I'm going with you because no person should go through saying goodbye to their brother alone. You don't have to be alone now, Spencer. You're not alone." He swallowed hard. "And, given the slight chance of seeing your father, I'd like to punch him in the throat, if that's okay."

I laughed for the first time in what felt like days.

"So stop asking me if I'm sure I want to fly across to the other side of the planet because there's nowhere else I'd rather be than with you. So finish packing... Or start." He gaped at my still-empty suitcase. "Jesus, Spencer, have you packed anything? We need to be there, like, soon!"

I literally grabbed three pairs of pants, five shirts, some jocks, and socks, folded them—kind of—and stuffed them into the suitcase. "Toiletries and I'm done."

"Just like that?"

"Yeah, why not?" I reached up to the back of the top shelf in my wardrobe and pulled out a metal safety box. I turned the key and picked out my passport and a black leather bracelet, leaving the other documents and papers, closed the lid, turned the key, and put it back.

"Uh, Spencer?" Andrew said, unsure. "I uh, I don't think leaving the key in the box is what they had in mind. You know, when they put a lock on it? So you could lock it? And take the key out of it?"

I snorted. "If they wanted, they could just take the whole box. There's nothing worth any money in there. I figure if the key is in it, if someone broke into my flat, they might take the time to look and see there's nothing of value in it instead of just stealing the whole thing. They have these specially built places for that kind of stuff these days called banks. Maybe you've heard of them." I laughed at his expression. "I just keep information and documents in there, that's all. The box is fireproof."

"Oh. You didn't need to be sarcastic about it."

"Yeah, I did." I pulled my shirt off and tossed it onto the bed and plucked out a clean button down shirt from my wardrobe. He was staring at my chest. Which reminded me. "Hey, you still need to draw me that tattoo."

He cleared his throat. "I know. I'm working on it."

"You are?"

"I've sketched a few ideas."

"Can I see them?"

His eyes widened. "Absolutely not. Not until it's finished."

"Any clues?"

"Nope."

I sighed, and when I was done doing up buttons, I started to roll my right sleeve. Slowly, one by one, I revealed the inked ravens, and my mood went back to sombre. "I asked Emilio about changing this blackbird." I ran my finger over the tattoo that had, for years, symbolised my brother Archer. "I was thinking of maybe changing this blackbird to a phoenix, but he wasn't sure it'd work. He took a stencil of it and was going to see what he could do. He didn't think it was gonna work out too well, but he'd try. See?" I pointed to the smallest of the blackbirds, "Its tail is wrong."

Andrew put his hand over the tattoo, the most loving of touches. "You could do a single piece on your back? A phoenix dedicated just for him? Keep the blackbird just as it is, because this tattoo"—he touched it lightly—"is part of who you are."

That made me smile. His total acceptance of my tattoos, encouragement even, made my chest warm. "I might do that actually."

Andrew put my passport in my breast pocket. "Did you call the doctor and ask him about you flying after your allergic reaction?"

"Um..."

He stared at me. "Spencer, you almost died two days ago from anaphylactic shock."

"I remember. I was there." My smile was slow spreading. "Of course I called him. I also asked him to email me information and permission notices to keep with my EpiPens when we travel. I also called the airline and inquired about their shellfish allergy policy." I kissed him softly. "I've done this before."

"I just worry, that's all."

"I know you do." I handed him the black leather bracelet. It looked like it could be a watch, but instead of a quartz face, this had a metal clasp.

"It's your medical alert bracelet," Andrew said softly, more to himself than to me. I held out my wrist, and Andrew secured it with care.

"Thank you."

He leaned in and kissed me. "You're welcome. Now get your toiletries. Lola will be here any—"

A loud knock interrupted. "Taxi to LAX," Lola's voice yelled.

"I'll get the door." Andrew disappeared, and I grabbed a few toiletries, threw another pair of shoes into my suitcase, and zipped it. I grabbed my backpack for a carry on, threw in a book, some headphones, the printed papers from the doctor, and two EpiPens.

Lola watched and waited for me to zip it until she hugged me. "I'm proud of you for doing this."

I nodded. "Me too."

Lola pulled back and looked at me with tears in her eyes. "Regardless of what happens over there, you're doing the right thing."

"This might be my one shot at having my brother in my life." I took a deep breath. "I have to try."

Andrew picked up my suitcase. "We need to go."

I looked at my watch. We really did. So, we grabbed my bags, then Andrew's bag from his car, and we loaded them into Cindy Crawford. Andrew gave his keys to Emilio and explained Sarah would be in to collect them. We said our goodbyes, and I didn't think much of it. But I got into the front passenger seat, Andrew climbed into the back. It wasn't a long drive, particularly when driven at warp speed. I guess I was so used to Lola's driving, no matter how much it still scared me, I learned that sudden lane changes and random ninety-degree turns were a given. But I glanced back at Andrew, and the look on his face...

He looked like he'd just met Impending Doom.

I almost laughed, but it wasn't funny. "Lola, slow it down."

"I'm not speeding," she said, then chanced a look in her rear vision mirror at Andrew. "Oh."

I turned in my seat to half face him. "Now you know what I mean. It kinda helps if you don't watch the road."

Lola brought Cindy Crawford to a screaming halt at the international terminal. I jumped out and held the door for Andrew. He was a little pale as he got out on mechanical legs. Lola already had our suitcases out on the pavement and hugged me fiercely. "I'll miss you," she said in my ear. "Take care. And remember, we'll all be here when you get back." Then she hugged Andrew. "Take care of him. And thank you for going with him."

She then raced around to the driver's side, jumped back into Cindy Crawford, and swerved into traffic. She waved at the people who honked.

"Sweet mother of God," Andrew mumbled. "I thought we were going to die."

"Her driving is... invigorating, yeah?"

He let out a low breath. "On the bright side, if the fourteen-hour flight ahead of us has the worst turbulence, it still can't be any worse than that."

Laughing, I grabbed our bags, and together we walked inside.

THEY SAY you can tell a lot about a person if you travel with them. Andrew was kinda stressed to begin with, but once we were checked in, boarded the plane, and settled into our seats, he was fine. He kept asking if I was okay, if I was nervous or hungry. But he was a wealth of calm and support, and even when the plane touched down in Sydney with too little sleep, his first concern was always for me.

Customs was both a blessing and a curse. It took a while, which was torture because Lewis was apparently picking us up from the airport. I wanted so badly to see him, but it also gave me time to gather my thoughts. I had no idea how this would go.

And that dreaded hope ballooned again in my chest. I was pretty sure it never went away. It was always waiting, lying dormant, but never gone. I wanted to have my brother in my life, with every fibre of my being. But I knew now, partly because of Andrew, partly because of Lola and Emilio, that I'd be okay if Lewis and I weren't able to bridge the gap between us. It was partly because of Aunt Marvie too, and partly because of me—she'd given me the strength to survive the worst of rejections—so I knew I would be okay.

But I still hoped.

I waited for Andrew to get through customs, and we walked out through the concourse together. I hadn't seen Lewis in years, and the last time I had seen him, he was just a kid. He was a man of twenty-three now, and I worried for a second that I wouldn't recognise him. Maybe he wouldn't recognise me... I certainly didn't have a beard or tattooed arms when my father told me the demise of our family was my fault for being gay. When Lewis and Archer had stood there, stunned and upset at my father's rage. Jesus, the look on their young faces...

Stepping foot back on Sydney soil sure brought with it memories I'd spent years trying to forget.

Andrew stopped. "Are you okay?"

I nodded. "Just memories."

I saw him then. A guy who looked just like me, only younger. No beard, but the eyes were mine and our mother's.

He stepped cautiously toward me. "Spencer?"

I nodded, my heart in my throat.

His eyes welled with tears, and he strode toward me, leaving the woman with him to follow. Lewis said nothing else, but he threw his arms around me and cried.

"I'm Andrew."

"Hi, Andrew. I'm Libby."

Lewis pulled away then, wiping his nose with an embarrassed laugh. Andrew and Libby were shaking hands. "Sorry, for leaving you to introduce yourselves. Libby, my brother, Spencer. Spencer, my girlfriend, Libby."

He called me brother.

"Lovely to meet you," I said, then I turned to Andrew. "Lewis, this is my boyfriend, Andrew. Andrew, Lewis."

Andrew shook his hand. "We spoke on the phone."

"Thank you for coming," Lewis said. "Both of you." He looked at me then, still a little teary but smiling. "It's so good to see you."

Libby put her arm around Lewis and smiled up at him, like he'd been as nervous as me. "We ready to go?"

I gave Andrew a relieved smile, then nodded to Libby. "Yeah."

And with our luggage in tow, the four of us walked out into a beautiful Sydney morning.

ELEVEN

WE PILED OUR BAGS INTO LEWIS'S AUDI, AND ANDREW and I got into the backseat. Lewis looked back at me. "Where to?"

"We're staying at Bondi. And I would love some sleep, but it's too early to check in. How about some breakfast?"

"Sounds great."

We found a little café that was the least busy out of all the eateries on the strip in Bondi. Andrew grabbed the backpack with the EpiPens like it was just part of what he did now. Which was kind of annoying and a whole lotta sweet. And maybe my last brush with shellfish had scared him *more* than he told me it did because he gave me a tight-lipped, no-arguments smile.

"Thank you," I said. But while he was fussing over backpacks and life-saving adrenaline shots, he missed the best kind of lifesavers. I turned him around. "Look."

Bondi Beach was world famous for very good reason. It was beautiful and so were the lifesavers who patrolled it. "Nice view, huh?"

"Not a bad view at all." He was totally looking at the two

lifesavers wearing nothing but tiny Speedos and big smiles.

"You're welcome," I joked, taking his hand and following Lewis and Libby into the café.

After we were seated, we ordered three coffees and a tea for me. I quizzed politely on the kitchen's protocol for allergies with their cooking and, after their complete reassurance, settled for a full breakfast of eggs, bacon, sausages, grilled tomato, and toast. Andrew ordered the same, citing, "Airplane food isn't great."

Lewis and Libby ordered as well, and Lewis handed over his credit card. When the waitress was gone, Lewis shook his head. "I forgot about your allergy to shellfish. I mean, I didn't *forget* forget. I guess I just hadn't thought of it in a while."

I gave him a smile. "That's okay. I try not to think of it either." Andrew stared at me disbelievingly, but bringing up my trip to hospital earlier this week probably wouldn't be a real good icebreaker. "So," I changed topics, "what's been going on in old Sydney town?"

Lewis told me about some of our old friends that I barely remembered and then about some cousins I hadn't thought of in years. I guess when you're kicked out of the family, it's not just immediate family you're removed from. Cousins got married, divorced, had babies, whatever.

He very deliberately didn't mention our parents, and that was fine with me.

They asked about LA and listened as we ate our meals. Lewis asked Andrew all about his job and was genuinely interested in what he did. It made me very happy that my brother was making an effort to get to know my boyfriend.

Then again, it was never Lewis who had the problem with me being gay.

Libby told us all about her studies in economics. Which surprised me, if I was being completely honest. She looked like she could be the poster girl for a surf brand or Colgate, but behind the model-looks was an incredibly intelligent woman. And it was very clear she adored Lewis.

Not once did we talk about Archer or my parents. It was a discussion we all knew was coming, but maybe we each wanted to enjoy this little slice of happiness before we dealt with reality and the horrible things that had, in turn, torn us apart and brought us back together again.

But even after Andrew's second cup of coffee, he still fought a yawn. "Sorry. Jet lag is not my friend. And you're telling me its Thursday? Because we left on Tuesday and I'm pretty sure there's supposed to be a day in between."

I sipped my tea seriously. "Wednesday's gone. There was a survey, and they decided to make it obsolete. There are no more Wednesdays."

Andrew snorted and rolled his eyes. "Right. I'm pretty sure if the survey was credible, it'd be Monday that people would get rid of."

"The poll was very close. But they figured then people would just hate Tuesdays. And it's not Tuesday's fault. And really, what purpose does Wednesday have? And what kind of word is Wednesday anyway?"

Andrew fought a smile. "You done?"

"I could go on for a while."

Lewis chuckled. "So, how long have you two been together?"

I looked at Andrew; he looked at me. "Um, just a few months."

"Really?" Libby said, her smile wide and somewhat disbelieving. "I could have sworn you two were together a few years, at least."

Andrew went a shade of red, and even his ears went pink. He cleared his throat. "Just two months."

Lewis eyed us like he couldn't figure something out, but before he said anything, I spoke first. "What about you guys?"

"Three years," Lewis answered.

"Almost three years," Libby corrected him. "We met at the Oaks. He was drunk and shamelessly charming."

"And she was stubborn. Wouldn't see me for weeks."

"Until he promised me the perfect date. If it wasn't perfect, he'd leave me alone."

"It was obviously perfect," Andrew said, waving his hand between them. "Because you're still together."

Lewis snorted. "Hardly. Libby ended up with food poisoning."

Libby grinned. "I vomited for two days, and Lewis here never left. He washed my clothes, my sheets, called my uni professors to organise notes because it was mid-years, and he made me toast and tea when I was well enough to eat."

"That's sweet," Andrew said. "Well, not the vomiting part."

Libby laughed. "It was. I figured if he'd seen me at my very worst and hadn't run for the hills, he had to be okay, right? We've been together since."

When Andrew yawned again, I knew it was time to go. "Okay, that's us. We need to bail for a few, if that's okay?"

"Of course." Lewis stood up. As we walked out, he asked, "Where are you staying?"

"The Atoll."

Lewis's gaze shot to mine, a look Andrew didn't miss. I shrugged and bit back a smile. Lewis studied me for a second but decided to leave whatever was on the tip of his tongue unsaid.

"You okay?" Andrew asked as we walked back to Lewis's car.

"I am." I looked over the blue of the Pacific and let out a

happy sigh. So far, all things were going well. It really did look like Lewis and I might just be okay. "I am."

It was only a short drive to the hotel, and truthfully, we could have walked it. But Lewis wanted to drive, so we didn't object. It wasn't exactly like he didn't know the way...

Lewis drove right up to the front doors and parked. He waved off the valet and opened the boot to his car, so Andrew and I could pull out our luggage. "We'll give you a few hours." Lewis glanced at his watch. "What if we come back at four?"

Instinctively, I looked at my watch. It was five hours away. "Sounds great." Before he got back into his car, I asked, "Um, can we go to the cemetery this afternoon?"

Lewis stopped and a sadness washed over his features. "Yeah. Of course."

I gave him the most reassuring smile I could manage. "Lewis, it's real good to see you."

Finally he smiled. "Likewise."

He and Libby drove off, and Andrew and I booked into our room. I handed over my credit card and signed, gladly took the key-card, and went to our room. Exhausted, we fell onto the bed.

Both of us still staring at the ceiling, Andrew reached blindly for my hand. "How do you feel?"

"Tired."

He laughed. "About Lewis. He seems genuine."

"He does."

"You look alike," Andrew said. "Minus the beard of course, and his hair is a little darker, but yeah, you're really alike."

"Is he hot?"

Andrew chuckled again but the sound died away. "You're still wary."

I turned my head to look at him, then. He was already

staring at me. "Of course I am. But he seems legit, yeah? Not like he's asked me here just to see how much hurt I can take?"

Andrew's eyes never left mine. "He seems like a guy who's desperate to reach out to the only brother he has left. There's a sadness in his eyes. And he watched you like he could hardly believe he was really seeing you. He's not acting, Spencer. He asked you here because he needs you."

I lifted his hand to my lips and kissed his knuckles. "Thank you."

He slow-blinked. "Sleep first. Just for a few hours. Then there will be sex. Just thought you should know."

I laughed and closed my eyes, feeling the weight of sleep luring me under. "Thank you for being here."

He rolled onto his side, pulled a pillow under his head, and closed his eyes. "Welcome."

I watched him sleep until my eyelids wouldn't cooperate any longer.

WHEN LEWIS PICKED us up at four, we were showered, changed, well-sated, and somewhat more human than we were at breakfast time. The afternoon was clear and warm; the sky was a blue I remembered from my childhood.

Lewis smiled at the bouquets we were holding, but never mentioned them. I guess he didn't need to. "You ready?" Lewis asked. He didn't want to know if I was ready to get in his car. He wanted to know if I was ready to see Archer's grave. Was anyone ever really ready to say goodbye?

I gave a nod, and Andrew joined me in the backseat of the car. Lewis slid in behind the wheel and Libby gave us a smile. "Sleep okay?"

"Yes, thank you," Andrew answered politely. And without another word spoken, Lewis drove us to Waverly Cemetery.

When we parked, Lewis and I walked side by side, and Libby and Andrew walked behind us. Lewis pointed the way, and I followed his lead. We'd walked a while, the small path a concrete vein that ran to the heart of the cemetery, when Lewis said, "It um… it was a nice service. It was private."

He turned onto a smaller capillary path, and he slowed his walk. He didn't need to point out which was Archer's. It was the newest one. I let out a long breath, trying to gather my thoughts.

Libby put her hand on Andrew's arm. "Shall we…?"

It was clear she wanted to give Lewis and I some alone time. Andrew looked at me questioningly, silently asking if he should go with her. I gave him a nod, and Andrew put his hand on the small of my back and kissed my cheek. "I won't be far away."

We watched them walk off, Andrew still holding one bouquet of flowers, as he and Libby walked toward the cliff edge. Waverly cemetery was world famous for its view over the Pacific. But my eyes were drawn back to the marble stone in front of me. Archer Cohen. I laid the flowers on the grave gently. "Hey brother. Been a while, huh?" I swallowed down the lump in my throat and took a step back. Lewis and I both took a few moments to breathe. "How did he die?"

Lewis answered in a whisper. "He hung himself."

I lowered my head and breathed through the burning weight in my chest. "When I asked you if it involved me, you said not directly. What did you mean?"

Lewis looked out across the cemetery. His eyes were filled with tears, but they remained unshed. "He left a note." Lewis shook his head then looked right at me. "He was gay."

And just like that, I felt like I had been punched in the heart.

"He said he knew our parents would never understand, and he couldn't reconcile the man they expected him to be with who he actually was. He couldn't... he couldn't live with their guilt and disappointment anymore."

"Oh, Jesus."

Lewis nodded and a tear rolled down his cheek. "He blamed them. And he told them that. He said they now had the death of two sons on their hands." His gaze bore into mine. "They considered you dead. Not him."

I took a shaky breath and my eyes welled with tears. This was too much. "He killed himself because he was gay?"

More tears streamed down Lewis's face. "No. He died because our parents made him feel worthless and dirty. Every time they sprouted some hateful speech about what made a man a real man, it must have just about killed him every time."

"Did you know he was gay?"

Lewis shook his head. "No. He never told me. He had girl-friends, or so I thought. We all thought." He wiped his face with his hands. "But in hindsight, looking back, I can join the dots. I can see now how he'd flinch or his jaw would bulge, or his eyes... I can see now how much he struggled." He let his head fall back and he groaned at the sky, trying to quell his emotions. "When you left—"

"When they kicked me out," I amended. "It was never my choice."

He put his hand up. "Sorry. When they kicked you out, he took it hard. Real hard. I mean we both did, but him especially. I just thought he was mostly upset because our own parents had just split up the only family we'd known. But he was twelve years old. He would have known he liked boys, and he would have been so fucking scared that if our parents found out they'd kick him out too."

"They wouldn't have understood."

Lewis slowly shook his head. "No. Even now after reading what he told them, they still don't get it. They think he's better off now..." More tears fell down his cheeks. "I fucking hate them, Spencer. I hate them."

I hugged him and held him while he cried. He pulled back, and with his jaw clenched he let out a growl. "I am so angry. I am pissed off for you, and I am so angry for Archie."

"Me too. I spent a long time angry, hurt, and confused. I still am, and I won't ever forgive them. But I could never change who I am."

"You shouldn't have to," he answered. "They should love you, just as you are. Parents should love their kids, right?"

"You'd think so."

Lewis let out a breath through puffed out cheeks. "You know what pisses me off the most? People feel sorry for our parents. They told everyone you were just an ungrateful teenager, a poor little rich kid who didn't like living with rules. Can you believe that? Then with Archie, it's all sympathy for them. Poor them." He shook his head angrily. "It's their fault. Every single thing that is fucked up with our family is their fault."

"What will you do?" I asked, my heart heavy. "I assume you work for the company."

He nodded. "Can I be completely honest with you?"

"Of course."

"What I intend to do is bide my time. The old man is a heart attack waiting to happen, and when that happens, I will gladly take his position as the sole remaining Cohen son in his prized Cohen & Sons Ltd. Then I will retract all the dona-tions he's made to those religious politicians for years and redirect it to every gay fundraiser in the state and dedicate every cent to my two brothers." He took a shaky breath. "And there won't be a damn thing he can do about it."

"You would do that?"

"Cheerfully. And whatever dividends I get, I'll halve with you. Spencer, you have to understand, whatever I get in their will, whenever that is, I will halve everything with you."

My smile was slow spreading but from my heart. "I appreciate that, but it's not necessary. I don't want their money. I don't need it. I have everything Aunt Marvie left to me, and that's more than I'll ever need."

"Ah," he nodded knowingly. "I wondered what pissed the old man off about that. He was livid for weeks."

I laughed at that. "That would explain the cease and desist I got."

He blanched. "The what?"

"It was the letter Archie gave me when he came to see me a year ago."

Lewis stared at me. "He never mentioned the letter. No wonder Dad didn't mind him going."

"He told you he saw me?"

"Yes. He said you wouldn't talk to him. He said you didn't need us."

I shook my head. "Lewis, there hasn't been a day that I haven't needed you. And I was a fucking mess when he showed up. I thought he was there to try and reconcile or something. But he didn't. He was awkward and nervous, like he didn't know what to say. He handed me the letter and walked out. I tried to get him to talk. I tried to go after him..."

Lewis patted my arm. "Know what I think? I think maybe he went to see you to see if he could make it on his own. Like, if you were doing okay, maybe he could be too, ya know?"

It was so much to think about. "Maybe. He never said

anything when he saw me in LA," I said, trying to get my head around everything. "I wish he had. If he just said something, I could have told him it'd be alright. He could have stayed with me. I would have done anything."

"You can't blame yourself," Lewis said, like this was an awful truth he knew only too well. "I can't blame me either. I don't blame Archie for doing what he did. I wish he didn't do it. God, I wish he'd told me he was gay. If only he'd told me, I could have told him he'd be alright too. I would have suggested he move to the States with you. If it would saved him. But the truth is, Spencer, it wouldn't have. The only thing that could have possibly saved him was our mother and father's love and acceptance. And that would never have happened. And that was a fact Archie knew too well. After all, he'd seen what they did to you." He let out a long breath. "I reckon he went over there to see, to tell you he was gay, and couldn't bring himself to admit it. But I guess we'll never know."

"How was he afterwards?" I asked. "When he got back?"

"Quiet. Withdrawn."

I scrubbed my hands over my face and fought the tears that threatened to spill. "Such a waste. Unnecessary and... God, Lewis, I wish I'd known."

He nodded, and for a long while, we stood in silence staring at the cold marble tombstone that now stood, an inadequate representation of the man who lay underneath it.

He was so much more than that.

The wind picked up, and it made me look around. The sky was changing colour, the sun in the western sky. Andrew and Libby weren't too far away, reading old tombstones.

"I could have sworn you and Andrew had been together for years," Lewis said, changing subjects. "The way you are with each other. It's like you've known each other forever."

I never took my eyes of Andrew. "He's the best thing that's ever happened to me."

"I can see that by how you look at him."

"He loves me," I said. Then I kinda laughed because it felt stupid to say that out loud. "And you wanna know what's fucked up?" Lewis looked at me, waiting for me to continue, but I kept my eyes on Andrew. "I can't tell him that I love him back. I want to, but I have... issues. I spent years in therapy after being disowned and rejected by my—our parents." I looked at Lewis then. "It fucks with your head. If it wasn't for my friends back home, Lola and Emilio, and now Andrew, and Aunt Marvie of course, then I'd be right here alongside Archie."

Lewis frowned. "Do you think you will one day?" he asked quietly. "Tell him, I mean."

I nodded. "I've come further in the last two months than I have in years. He's been better for me than he can ever know. I know I will, one day, I just hope he can wait that long."

"I'm sure he will." He took a deep breath and smiled. "I was serious about splitting dividends and inheritances with you. Will you consider it?"

"Whatever you would have given me, set up a foundation instead, in Archie's name. Honour him, for young, homeless LGBTIQ people. For those who have no hope left."

Lewis smiled genuinely. "The Archer Cohen Foundation. I like the sound of that. I wouldn't know where to start though." His brow furrowed.

I smiled as Andrew and Libby started walking back toward us. "Andrew's parents run a similar thing in LA. I can get you a complete business model."

"For real?"

"I could help you from LA. With information and business plans or whatever you need."

Lewis was grinning now, excited. "I would really like that."

Andrew smiled as he got closer. Maybe my smile made him happy. It was then I noticed he was still holding the flowers. "Lewis?" I asked. "Do you know where Aunt Marvie was buried?"

"Oh, of course," he said. "I should have offered. It's this way."

We followed Lewis and Libby, and Andrew took my hand. He was looking at me as we walked, and I could see the unasked questions in his eyes. I gave him a smile and squeezed his hand that I hoped he understood was me saying I was okay.

"It's just up here." Lewis nodded the direction and stopped at a simple white marble grave. There were no flowers, and I wondered if there ever had been. I made a mental note to organise monthly deliveries of her favourite roses.

I read the name engraved in stone. "Marion Cohen."

The dates pronounced her seventy-five years of age when she passed and her favourite lines of her favourite song. The very line I had tattooed on my arm above the roses.

I lifted the sleeve of my T-shirt to show Lewis. "She always loved that line." I couldn't help but smile. "'Running where even the brave wouldn't go.' That's her." My eyes welled with tears. "She was the bravest person I knew."

Andrew put his arm around me in that silent, pillar-of-strength way he did so well.

The marble tombstone was beautiful, and I had no doubt she would have had every detail worked out long before she died. But one thing was missing. "If the word *mother* means one who cares for, loves, provides for, and encourages, then she was mine. She didn't give me life, but in a way she did. It saddens me that people who walk past won't know she was loved. It should say 'Beloved mother of Spencer.'"

Andrew handed me the bouquet and I stepped forward and put the roses across her grave. "I think of you every day," I told her. "I still drink green tea every day in your honour. I still play those records you loved. I still cook your favourite recipes. I am who I am because of who you allowed me to be, and I will be forever grateful." I let my tears fall, not ashamed to cry. "She loved me, when no one else did."

Andrew stood behind me, put his hand on my waist, and rested his forehead against my shoulder. Without a word, he let me know I wasn't alone. I turned and he pulled me against him, holding me tight. He put his hand around my neck and kissed the side of my head. I breathed him in, revelling in that safety, that warmth I found in his arms.

Keeping one arm around Andrew, I looked at Lewis. He and Libby were standing back a bit, both teary eyed. "Did she have a funeral service?"

He nodded. "It was only a graveside service."

That made me smile. "She hated churches."

"There were a lot of people."

"I wish I'd known."

Lewis frowned. "You have every right to be mad for not being told. I wish I'd have told you. I should have, and I'm sorry."

"It's not you I'm mad at," I told him.

"It's such a fucked up mess, isn't it?" Lewis whispered. "Everything."

I took a deep breath and let it out slowly. "You know what? It is. Everything up until today, that is. But we can start over from now, yeah? You and me, we're good, right?"

Lewis scrubbed his hands over his face, wiping away the

last of his tears. He barked out a laugh and nodded. "I'd like that, very much."

I let go of Andrew and hugged my brother. It didn't strip away years of hurt between us, but it was a bloody good start. He squeezed me hard before patting my back and pulling away. His whole face was smiling. "You guys hungry? I'm starving. How about we go grab an early dinner?"

I slipped my arm around Andrew once more, so thankful for him being here. "You wanna eat?" I asked him.

"You know me," he answered. "I'm always hungry."

I smiled at Lewis. "Sounds great."

As we walked back to the car, Lewis asked, "Can I ask you something?"

I shrugged. "Sure."

"Why are you staying at the Atoll?"

I grinned at him. "Well, ya see, I thought we could stay somewhere else and give income to a competitor rather than give my father one cent of my money. But then I realised the opportunity for me to sleep with a man in one of his beds was just too good an opportunity to let go."

Lewis paused and stared at me over the roof of his car. Then he threw his head back and laughed. "Oh my God, that is the funniest thing I've heard all day."

We all climbed into the car, and Andrew was clearly confused. "One of your father's beds?"

"The Atoll chain of hotels," I answered simply. "My father owns them."

Andrew's mouth fell open. "Oh."

Lewis snorted as he pulled out into traffic. "If he knew you were staying at the Bondi Atoll with a guy, he'd bust a vessel in his forehead."

I laughed and lifted Andrew's hand to my lips. "And that is the reason I did it."

TWELVE

THE RESTAURANT LIBBY CHOSE FOR DINNER LOOKED over the northern end of Bondi Beach. Lewis parked at the hotel, and we walked up, dressed just as we were. It was casual, laidback, and lovely.

We had a few drinks and a few laughs; the mood between us was one of relief and happiness. Something I got the feeling Lewis hadn't experienced for a while. And if I ever thought for one moment that my being disowned didn't affect my brothers, I was wrong. Archer had struggled so terribly with his own secrets that he could no longer bear the weight of them, and Lewis had suffered alone.

Yes, my world had been turned upside down, and I'd been disregarded like garbage. But I had Aunt Marvie. I had someone who took me in and showed me what unconditional love was. My brothers didn't have that.

I was starting to think I got the better deal.

Lewis raised his glass. "To new beginnings."

We all clinked glasses and toasted. "To new beginnings."

Lewis sipped his drink. "You know, after Archie's funeral, I went straight home and called your solicitor. It took a few calls because I couldn't remember his name. I remember Dad having a shitfit over Aunt Marvie's will, and there were a lot of solicitors involved. But I found him and asked him to forward on the news of Archie. When two days passed, I called him back and he said he'd spoken to you and given you my contact details. I thought you were done with this family, ya know? I wouldn't have blamed you one bit, but I had to try."

"It was a long two days," Libby said, looking fondly at Lewis. "He jumped every time the phone rang."

"Spencer was in the hospital," Andrew said before I could explain.

"You what?" Lewis asked, his smile now a look of concern.

I tried to play it down. "Yeah, I um, had a bit of a run in with some unexpected crab meat."

Andrew didn't play it down at all. "He almost died. The doctor said the allergic reactions are getting worse, and the next one could be his last. It was the scariest thing I've ever seen."

"You were there?" Lewis asked.

"Thankfully," I answered. "We were at his parents' house. I was dancing rock 'n' roll, 50s style with his mum and then we"—I motioned between Andrew and me—"slow danced to Ray Charles, and then I collapsed on their living room floor. Andrew and his dad saved my life."

"This was on Sunday?" Lewis asked quietly. I nodded. "Jesus. I almost lose you the day we buried Archie." Lewis blinked several times, like he couldn't compute what he was saying.

"And you flew here just days after?" Libby asked. She looked as stunned as Lewis.

"Of course. Lewis asked me to." I shrugged and gave her a

smile. I could feel Lewis looking at me, but I couldn't return the eye contact. It had been such an emotional day, and quite frankly, I was sick of crying.

"Well," Libby said. "I'm glad you're here. Both of you." She included Andrew.

"I'm glad I'm here too," Andrew said. He squeezed my hand on my thigh.

I lifted our joined hands to set them on the table and threaded my fingers with his. "Me too."

Lewis put his arm around Libby. "So, Andrew, Spencer was telling me your parents run a foundation for people in need?"

"Yes. The Acacia Foundation is my mother's third child."

Lewis explained our earlier conversation about possibly setting up some kind of centre for LGBTIQ kids, with all funding coming from what would have been Archie's and my dividends of my father's company.

We ate our dinner and drank more wine, talking non-stop about anything and everything. And as I sat there with my brother and Libby and Andrew at my side, I couldn't help but think how surreal it was. If I could stop time and look at this moment, to soak it all in, I would highlight this moment as perfect. My brother, who I'd never expected to see again, let alone have his full acceptance and friendship, and Andrew, the man I loved... Like I said. It was perfect.

We decided to call it a night and walked back to the hotel, saying our goodbyes, and Lewis said he'd see us in the morning. When Andrew and I made it back into our room, he fell dramatically on his back on the bed. "I'm exhausted."

I lifted his left leg and pulled off his shoe, then did the same to his right before crawling over him and softly kissing him. "How exhausted?"

His smile was slow spreading. "Not that exhausted."

"Good." I kissed him deeper, more thoroughly. I waited until he moaned, then pulled my mouth from his. I sat back so I could pull his shirt over his head. I tossed it onto the floor, and he flipped me onto my back like I weighed nothing, my head on the pillows, and he settled his weight between my open legs. He kissed me deeply, tilting his head for the perfect angle, his tongue invaded my mouth.

Right then.

Bossy Andrew was back.

He only stopped kissing me to undress me, and even that was too long. My swollen lips needed his like I needed air. When we were naked, he lay on top of me, our cocks aligned, and he fisted us both. But it wasn't what I wanted... No, not what I *needed*.

I took his face in my hands and whispered, "Make love to me."

His eyes fluttered closed, and I felt a shiver run through him. But he did as I asked, slowly and surely getting me ready for him to the point where I was begging him. "Andrew, please. I need you inside me."

In the moonlit room, with his pupils blown with lust, his lips kiss-swollen, he was the most beautiful I'd ever seen him. He sat back on his haunches and rolled on a condom, applied more lube, and aligned his cock at my arsehole. He fell forward onto one arm and pushed inside me. His eyes drifted shut, but I gripped his face and made him look at me. He thrust into me slowly, filling me, stretching me, and I watched every emotion flicker in his eyes.

And just like that, we made love. The slowest of movements, the gentlest of touches, the softest, sweetest kisses.

He filled me so completely. The most perfect jigsaw puzzle, the missing piece of me. I loved him, and when the words were on the tip of my tongue, he kissed me.

I didn't say them out loud, but I'm fairly certain he could taste them.

We fell asleep in each other's arms, an emotional end to an emotional day.

I WOKE up when Andrew came back in through the balcony sliding-glass door. He was showered, dressed, and looking decidedly awake and not in bed with me. "Hey," I said, my voice croaked with sleep.

He smiled brightly. "Hey, sleepyhead."

"Whatcha doing?"

"Taking photos of the beach to send to Lola and Sarah. I've ordered breakfast. Go shower and get dressed. It's almost nine."

I rolled onto my back and rubbed my eyes. "Shit. I must have been tired. I don't think I even stirred."

Andrew smiled. "Yesterday was a draining day for you. I'm not surprised."

I sat on the edge of the bed, not a stitch of clothing on, and scratched my head, ignoring the ache in my arse. "Well, there's that and your Cockness Monster."

Andrew burst out laughing, turning red from his forehead to his collar. He pointed to the bathroom. "Shower."

I chuckled as I walked into the en-suite. The shower was hot and felt great against the muscles in my neck and shoulders. I didn't even notice that Andrew must have come in at some point, but when I got out of the shower, the door was shut and my clothes were folded neatly on the bathroom cabinet. I pulled on the navy knee-length denim shorts and striped T-shirt, fixed my hair, and when I opened the door, I saw the reason why Andrew had shut the door.

Lewis sat on the bed, picking through what looked like room-service breakfast. Andrew sat at the table, sipping his coffee. They were both smiling at something I'd missed.

I looked pointedly at the tray of food and Lewis. "Hey. Enjoying my breakfast?"

He wiped his fingers on the serviette. "Yep. You need more bacon."

I snorted out a laugh and poured myself a green tea. I plonked myself in the other chair opposite Andrew. "Tea's good. Thank you."

He pulled a piece of toast apart and bit into it. "Welcome."

Lewis helped himself to a glass of water. "So, what's the plan for today?"

"I thought I'd take Andrew down to the beach. Can't come to Bondi and not actually set foot on Bondi. What about you?"

Lewis shrugged. "I've taken this week off work. That was even before I knew you were coming. I can be your taxi all day if you want?"

"Sounds good." I sipped more of my tea and ate half a piece of toast while I pulled on my shoes. Given I was only wearing a T-shirt, Lewis could see my tattooed arms, and I caught him looking at the individual pictures, but he didn't ask about them. And I was kinda glad. Yesterday was all about the past and things we wished we could change. I wanted today to be about moving forward, and I kinda got the feeling he did too. "We good to go?"

Leaving the tray of breakfast at the door, we stepped into the elevator. Lewis pressed the button to the lobby. "So, this might be TMI, and it really is none of my business, but I certainly hope you gave one of father dearest's hotel beds a gay old christening it won't ever forget."

I laughed as the elevator doors opened. "Believe me, if it was memory foam, the next people would be in for a treat."

Andrew groaned. "Spencer!"

Lewis busted up laughing as we walked out into the warm Sydney morning. I shrugged at Andrew and grinned at my brother. "It's like we're fourteen and sixteen all over again." Lewis laughed, and I felt lighter than I had in years. I put my arm around Andrew's shoulder. "Come on down to the water. Let's see if that Cockness Monster of yours can swim."

Lewis scoffed. "His what?"

"Never mind," Andrew answered, and with a hard shove, pushed me into the wall. "You're not funny."

I was laughing too hard to give him a witty comeback, so I grabbed his hand and crossed the street instead. Lewis shook his head at us, obviously not getting the joke, but he was still grinning. This was where we'd grown up. Technically we'd visited Bronte Beach more, but we'd spent many summer days at Bondi. It was fitting that, out of all the places in Sydney Lewis and I could be catching up, it was here. We headed to the northern end of the beach where the locals went. Most tourists went to the southern end but we went straight to Flat Rock. We took off our shoes and walked along the rocky outcrop where the waves met land.

"I can see why they called it Flat Rock," Andrew said, looking over the huge area of, ironically enough, flat rock.

"Yeah, we don't try too hard to name stuff here," Lewis replied.

Andrew chuckled at that, and I just happened to catch a glimpse of him as the breeze and sea mist washed over him. Kids were jumping into the water behind us, laughing before they disappeared into the ocean, the sun was warm, the sky a vivid blue. "Not a bad view," Andrew said, looking out over the Pacific.

"Not bad at all," I agreed quietly, looking at nothing but him. He blushed shyly.

"Come on, up this way," Lewis said, calling us over to the long stairs that fringed the rocky cliff. "Remember this?" he asked, leading the way.

Did I ever. I climbed the too-many, too-steep stairs too damn quick and was breathless when I got to the top. Lewis was no better but Andrew was barely breathing hard. He clapped my shoulder. "You need to start coming to the gym with me."

I sat my arse on a railing and waved him off. Lewis sat beside me, and we watched as Andrew walked over to the outdoor gym equipment. It was very popular with the locals, an outdoor workout area overlooking Bondi Beach, though it was more a competition spot between buff gym junkies trying to look better, be bigger, and fitter than the next guy.

A couple of guys looked at Andrew, and I could see them sniggering, thinking that this geeky looking guy was gonna be good for nothing but a laugh. There they were shirtless, all tanned and muscular, and Andrew was pale, wearing a shirt with his argyle vest over top. But then Andrew jumped up and gripped the chin-up bar, and crossing his heels, he proceeded to lift himself effortlessly. Not just a few times slowly, but he must have done twenty in rapid succession, and he did them easily.

The two guys were now watching him with *oh-shit* written on their faces, though Andrew was completely oblivious. He let go of the bar and grinned at me as he wiped his hands on his shorts. Then he pulled his T-shirt sleeves up to his shoulders and stood between two parallel bars. He expertly jumped up, his biceps bulged, and he lifted his legs to ninety-degrees and held it. For about a freakin' minute. His shoulder muscles were stretching his shirt, and his arms were straining, then with a laugh, he let go and shook himself out. He walked back over to us, like he'd done nothing spectacular. "Well, that's my work out for today."

Lewis elbowed me in the ribs. "Close your mouth."

I chuckled. "Jesus, Andrew. I really should go to the gym with you." Then I nodded to where those two guys who had been watching him were. "You should take your shirt off and show those guys what you've got going on under that vest."

Andrew looked around and quickly turned back. He went a full shade of red. "Were they watching?"

I snorted. "Oh, Andrew. You have no idea."

Then Lewis's phone rang. He fished it out of his pocket and groaned. I saw the name on the screen, whether he wanted me to see it or not.

Dad.

Lewis let out a long sigh. "Sorry." He answered the call, and thankfully I could only hear his end of the conversation. "I told you I wasn't coming in this week. ... Just down at the beach. ... Can't Chris look after it?" He groaned again. "Fine. I'll be there in twenty minutes."

He disconnected the call and his nostrils flared. "Sorry about that. I have to go into work."

"No worries," I told him. "We'll catch up tonight, yeah?"

Lewis nodded. "Sounds good." He stood up, then stopped. He took out his car keys. "Here. Take my car. Show Andrew the sights of Sydney."

"I don't have a licence anymore. It expired," I told him.

He threw the keys to me. "Then don't get caught." And with that, he walked down to Campbell Parade, hailed a cab, and was gone.

I jingled the keys. "Well, then. Where to first?"

He tried not to cringe. "You're going to drive your brother's new Audi after you've not driven for how many years?"

I held the keys out. "You wanna try?"

"God, no."

I laughed at his expression, and we walked back to the hotel. I was stupidly excited at the thought of driving again. It had been years. I'd never driven in the States, and when I got behind the wheel and started the engine, it purred like a kitten, and I grinned like an idiot. "When we get home, back to LA, I think I'd like to get my licence."

He chuckled at me. "Just don't sideswipe anything."

"Oh ye of little faith." I slipped the car into reverse and neatly pulled out of the park. I was cautious and nervous, but mostly excited, and it really was a skill you just didn't forget. I merged cleanly into the flow of traffic on Campbell Parade and headed toward the city. As we got to a familiar intersection, I realised there was something I needed to see. "Before I give you the grand tour, there's something I want to show you first."

I drove up a few streets then turned up the street of my childhood and pulled the car to the kerb. I pointed to the pretentiously large double storey white house up a bit further. "That's the house I grew up in."

Andrew stared at it. "You never told me your family owned hotels."

"Up until two days ago, I didn't have a family."

Andrew shot me an apologetic look. "Sorry. You know what I mean though."

"I do. It just wasn't anything worth talking about. I try not to mention them or even think about them, to be honest."

Andrew nodded in understanding. I looked back at the house, just as the garage door opened. My heart stopped, not knowing who I would see, if they'd see me, and if they did, what they would do.

A new model BMW backed down the drive and stopped. The garage roller door lowered, and a woman I'd never seen before got out of the car and collected her mail from the mailbox.

"Who's that?"

"I don't know." I studied the house some more and realised the four big pots that my mother had paid a fortune for were no longer across the front balcony, and there was a dog in the front yard and my mother was allergic to dogs... The woman driving the BMW drove past, and it was then we saw she had two small kids in the back. "They must have sold it and moved."

Andrew frowned and squeezed my hand. Maybe he was going to reason that surely my parents would have told me, until he remembered that no, they certainly wouldn't have. "You okay?"

Was I okay? I took a second to assess how I felt in my heart, looking for the most honest answer I could find. "You know what? I am. I am fine. This hasn't been my home for almost ten years. And as for my parents? I don't give one single fuck about where they live now."

Andrew smiled at me. "Will you show me where your Aunt Marvie lived?"

I grinned at him. "I'd love to." I pulled the car back into the street and drove past the house that had been my child-hood home. The fact I didn't feel anything was a very welcome realisation that maybe I was finally moving on and accepting of how my parents had treated me. I also knew damn well the man sitting in the car with me had a lot to do with that.

Maybe that was the difference between Andrew and therapy. My therapy had focused so much on my parents and the hurt they'd caused, whereas Andrew, very unknow-ingly, had focused on me. He showed me that I was someone worth loving, and that if I could just lower my walls a little, it would not only let love in, but also let some of the hurt out.

I drove through the backstreets of Double Bay and pulled up out the front of a rather large bungalow style house. "This was us here."

"Does it back onto the water?"

"Yep."

"Jesus."

I barked out a laugh. "Now you know why my father had a shitfit about Aunt Marvie's will."

I could see it in his eyes when it slowly dawned on him. "She left you this house?"

I nodded slowly. "I sold it. Hence the money."

He stared at the house, then back at me. "You said she left you a chunk of change."

I shrugged. "Your folks live in a ritzy part of town too, ya know. You never told me their house was a mansion."

"I said they were in theatre."

"Yes, but so are starving actors. LA is full of them."

He laughed. "When you said you didn't need to work, I thought... well, I didn't know what I thought, to be honest."

"I have it tied up in term deposits and invested in stock, so if you saw my bank account, you would think I was just kinda doing okay. My portfolio, on the other hand, is fairly decent."

He looked at me for a long second, then snorted out a disbelieving laugh. "You are the most modest person I've ever met."

I shrugged. "My great-grandfather had made some very smart real estate investments in the 30s, which my whole family, aunts and uncles, benefited from when he died. My parents were name-droppers, social-ladder climbers. You know the type. But Aunt Marvie was very humble, very down to earth, regardless of her financial worth. She taught me to treat everyone the same, whether it's the CEO of a bank or the guy who cleans the toilets."

Andrew was smiling warmly at me. "I wish I could have met her."

I leaned across the console of the car and waited for him to do the same so I could kiss him. "Thank you."

Andrew sat back in his seat. "Can I ask you something?"

"Of course."

"Do you regret selling it?"

"Nope. Sydney isn't my home anymore. I wasn't ever coming back here."

He looked out the window at the house, like he didn't want to see my face when he asked, "What will you do now? Now that you and Lewis are talking?"

"I'll go back to LA and talk to him from there." I squeezed Andrew's hand. "Look at me." He did and I continued. "My home is in LA. With Emilio and Lola, and there's this pretty amazing guy I'm seeing. He's on the cover of *The World's Most Incredible Boyfriends* and everything."

He fought a smile. "Is he now?"

"Yep. And the *Sexiest Man Alive, Cockness Monster* edition. It was a sell-out, just flew off the shelves."

Now he laughed. "You're absurd."

"And you're kinda perfect. So we're even." I kissed him, both of us smiling, and started driving again. I turned onto the main arterial road and followed the signs to the city.

"Where to first?" Andrew asked.

"First stop today on the amazing Spencer Cohen's Sydney sightseeing tour is the glorious city centre where we shall take in Darling Harbour, Circular Quay, the Rocks, and a little thing called the Opera House. Then, we shall venture over the Harbour Bridge, and if we have time, we'll take the handsome American tourist to the zoo to meet some of Australia's cute and cuddly wildlife."

"Aren't they all dangerous?"

"Not all. Some will kill you, the rest will just seriously injure or maim you. You'll be fine."

Andrew laughed at me. "You know, you're actually a pretty good driver." He held out his hand, which I took, grateful Lewis had an automatic car.

I rested our joined hands on my thigh. "Thanks."

FLYING out of Sydney felt both good and bad. We'd had a great few days with Lewis and Libby, and while I was looking forward to going home, I was sad to be leaving my brother. He and Libby had driven us to the airport and come to see us off.

He hugged me hard before reluctantly letting me go. "We'll talk, yeah?"

I nodded. "Absolutely. Email, phone, whatever."

He looked a bit upset at the goodbye, but like me, glad we had bridged the gap between us. "I really can't thank you enough for coming. It... it means a lot."

"Next time you guys'll have to come visit us."

Lewis's eyes lit up. "Can we? That'd be great. Libby's got two weeks off in October, and we were wondering if we should go away."

"Just book the tickets and let me know when to pick you up."

Lewis was much happier knowing there would definitely be a next time. He hugged Andrew goodbye, and when Libby hugged me, she whispered in my ear, "Thank you. For everything. He needed this."

"So did I," I whispered back to her. Then I kissed her cheek. "Anytime."

THEY CALLED OUR FLIGHT, and Andrew and I both fell into our seats, exhausted. Knowing we'd be on a plane all night, we'd spent the day doing everything we could think of, including spending half the night in bed doing everything *but* sleeping. We'd been shopping for everyone we knew, and we'd eaten our own body weights in food.

But I knew as soon as I sat in that plane seat, I'd be dozing off to sleep. With my head on the headrest, I turned to look at Andrew. "Thank you for coming with me."

He looked just as tired as I felt. His smile was slow and one-sided. "You're very welcome."

All I could do was stare at him. Someone asked him a question, but I couldn't pay attention. I couldn't draw my eyes away. He was so fucking perfect. Unbelievably gorgeous, kind, intelligent, and funny. If I were to believe that souls were split in two and we needed to search out our soulmate, then I'd found him. He was the very missing half of me.

"Spencer?" Andrew must have asked me something. "A drink? The attendant wants to know if you want a soda or water. They don't have green tea; I've already asked, and I doubt the pot of tea would be good enough—"

"I love you."

He stopped rambling and stared at me. "What?"

I was still leaning tiredly against the headrest, smiling at him. "I said I love you."

"Oh." He put his hand to his mouth. The flight attendant gushed some *awwww* sound, and the woman next to Andrew stared at him, waiting for his response. "Spencer..."

"I've been trying to say those words for weeks. You know it's hard for me, but you're pretty fucking incredible, you know that?"

Andrew blinked back tears, and he mouthed, *I love you too* like his voice wouldn't work.

I smiled sleepily at him. "Just thought you should know."

Andrew waved the attendant off, and she smiled at how flustered he was. He took a deep breath and slid his hand over mine. "If there was a magazine called *The Most Awkwardly Romantic Declarations Of Love*, I'm pretty sure that would be on the cover."

I chuckled. "Sorry. I told you I had a stupid heart and even stupider brain. They just kinda decide these things on their own."

He laughed, and his eyes glistened with happy tears. "I love you too," he whispered, getting actual words out this time, and leaned over for a quick kiss.

I sighed, like his words were a warm blanket. "Now I can sleep."

"Sleep? How can I sleep? My heart is doing this allegro thing right now, and I feel like I've been injected with caffeine. You can't just say you love me and expect me to sleep."

I closed my eyes, still facing him in my seat, still holding his hand. I'm pretty sure my smile wasn't going away anytime soon. "Shhhh."

I could feel him glaring at me. "Ugh. I hate you."

Now I laughed, nearly asleep. "No you don't."

He raised our joined hands, and I felt his lips against the back of my hand. "No, I really don't."

THIRTEEN

THERE'S SOMETHING TO SAY ABOUT COMING HOME. Landing in LA was a relief I could feel in my bones. We had managed a few hours sleep, but the time zones scrambled my already-tired brain. "What day is it?"

Andrew looked at me blankly. "I have no clue."

We got through customs in a zombie-like haze and walked out to find both Lola and Sarah waiting for us. It was so good to see Lola, and I quickly scooped her up for a bear hug.

Andrew hugged his sister too. "I wasn't expecting you."

"Well, we"—Sarah gave a pointed look at Lola—"thought it might be safer if we both turn up. You know, your first trip away, not the happiest of circumstances." She frowned at me. "We weren't sure if you'd be sick of each other, and we thought we'd come to, you know, offer support."

Lola made a face. "It sounded like a better idea on the phone."

Sarah laughed. "Yeah, it kinda did."

"Sick of each other?" I asked, looking at Andrew and shrugged.

"Thought never crossed my mind," Andrew replied. He

looked at his sister. "What day is it?" She just laughed and took his suitcase. He didn't move. "No, I'm being serious."

"Oh, it's Sunday."

"Thank God," Andrew mumbled and rolled his neck. "I don't go back to work till Wednesday." Then he squinted at her. "Sunday? Really?"

He wasn't joking when he said he didn't cope with jet lag. Sarah said, "I thought I'd take you home and get all your laundry done while you did your jet-lag, dying thing."

Andrew looked at me. "Oh."

Lola put both hands on his shoulders and peered up into his eyes. "You want to spend more time with Spencer, don't you?"

"Well, I just, yeah..." He looked kinda lost. "Um, Sunday? Really? We left Australia on Sunday."

I put my arm around his shoulder and pulled him against me, trying not to laugh. I looked at both Sarah and Lola. "We'll go back to his place. Do laundry and sleep." I looked at Lola. "Then we'll do dinner at the tattoo shop so we can tell you all about the trip. How does that sound?"

Lola did her little jumpy-clap thing. "Perfect!" She grabbed my suitcase, and she and Sarah walked ahead while I followed, with Andrew tucked under one arm. I felt like a different man than the one that left here just a few days ago. In a lot of ways, I guess I was. I kissed the side of Andrew's head as the warmth of the LA sun washed over me.

Thankfully, it was Sarah driving Andrew's car, not Lola in Cindy Crawford. I wasn't quite up for jet lag *and* heart palpitations. We dropped Lola off with promises to see her later, and Sarah drove us to Andrew's. When we walked in, Andrew left his suitcase near the hall that led to the laundry. He put his arms out and let his head fall back. "Ugh. Home."

"I bought food for you," Sarah said. She looked right at

me. "Andrew's never dealt with jet lag, and I knew he wouldn't have the patience for ordering in, so I did it for you. It's just some pasta. I thought the carbs would help you sleep. You just need to heat it."

"You are an angel," I told her. "Leave the laundry, though. Seriously. We can deal with that later. You hungry?"

Sarah looked at her watch. Apparently it was mid-morning. Felt like dinnertime. She shrugged. "Sure, why not?"

I guided Andrew to the kitchen and leant his arse against the counter before Sarah and I fixed some food. With three bowls of a mix of pastas, we talked about our trip. Well, I talked, Andrew squinted a lot, his brain obviously somewhere else. I gave Sarah a diluted version of what happened with Lewis; how I said goodbye to one brother, and through his tragic loss, gained my other brother back. I told her how I took Andrew sightseeing and showed her some photos on my phone of him holding a koala. "Aww, that's the cutest thing ever," she said.

Andrew stared at her. "How can it be Sunday? How is it physically possible to arrive before our departure time?"

Sarah laughed and patted his arm. She looked at me. "Take him to bed. His brain will catch up on the whole time-zone thing after some sleep." She put the dirty dishes in the sink and kissed Andrew's cheek. "It's good to have you home." Then she smiled at me. "Both of you."

I took Andrew's hand, and when we'd said goodbye to Sarah, I took Andrew straight upstairs. I put him to bed, taking his shoes off, then I thought better of it and pulled his jeans off too. I stripped as well and climbed in beside him, sinking into his heavenly soft bed. Sarah was right. All that pasta in my belly was putting me to sleep. I closed my eyes and was drifting off to sleep when Andrew spoke. "You told me you loved me."

I opened my eyes to find him looking at me. "I did. I do."

He sighed and smiled. "Tell me again."

I rolled on top of him, spreading his legs apart with my knees and settling between his thighs. I put my hands to his face and pushed his hair back and watched as his eyes swam. I kissed him softly at the same time I rubbed my erection along his. "I love you. Andrew Landon, I am *in* love with you. I have been in love with you since that time at my place when I asked you to pick an album to play, and out of all of my vinyl collection, you picked Jeff Buckley's 'Hallelujah.' I just haven't been able to tell you, until now. You healed something inside me."

A single tear ran from the corner of his eye to his temple. "Oh."

I kissed him again, and this time he opened his mouth. He tilted his head and deepened the kiss while his fingers dug into my back and his hips rolled into mine. He only stopped kissing me to breathe. He bit his lip. "I read somewhere that sex cures jet lag."

"Is that so?"

"Yep. Getting fucked into the mattress. It's the only way."

I laughed but was only too happy to oblige.

AFTER CURING Andrew's jet lag, we slept for a few hours, did laundry, which we took back to my place, then made our way down to Emilio's shop. As soon as we walked in through the door, Emilio stopped disinfecting his work station and hugged me. "Here they are!"

"Man, it's good to see you," I told him. "How's it been?"

Emilio and Daniela closed up shop for the day while he filled me in on the happenings of the tattoo shop. We put an order in for dinner to be delivered, and Lola and Gabe arrived, as did the Chinese food, right on cue.

It was perfect.

The most important people in my life, not including Lewis and Libby, surrounded me and listened intently as I told them about everything that happened in Sydney. We ate our dinner, sitting around Emilio's waiting room, like we'd always done. Only now Andrew sat beside me, our little group perfectly paired off.

"Oh," I said, looking at Emilio. "Andrew had the idea of a single piece tattoo for Archer's phoenix. He thought maybe leaving this one"—I nodded to the blackbird on my arm—"just as it is. He said it tells its own story. I kinda like that."

"Awesome." Emilio smiled at Andrew. "Great idea."

"I was thinking about making the phoenix a back piece. But we can work on the perfect one, no rush."

Emilio gave me a nod. "It would be my honour to draw that for you."

"Oh," Daniela said. "Andrew, weren't you supposed to be working on something for Spencer?"

"Yes!" I said. "He reckons he's half done it or got some rough idea or something."

Andrew cleared his throat. "I finished it, actually."

He what? "You did? When?"

Andrew blushed a little and looked at me sheepishly. "On the plane. I couldn't sleep, and the cabin was kinda dark, so I took a pen to the back of the airline safety manual."

I would have found that funny if I wasn't so intrigued. "What did you draw?"

He swallowed hard and his lip pulled down on one side. "I um, I have it here." He pulled out his wallet and took out a folded piece of paper. "I'd need to do it properly. This is just a general idea. But you wanted me to draw the one thing that symbolises who you are. What I think of when I think of you."

With a deep breath, he handed the piece of paper to me.

It was an elephant. He'd only had a pen to draw with, but he used the simple writing tool like a paintbrush. Inside the elephant was a pattern of leaves and circles, so intricately done, all different depths of blue... It was incredible.

Andrew must have taken my lack of words as though I didn't like it, because he started that nervous, fast-talking thing. "You wanted me to draw something that comes to mind when I think of you. And I... well, I don't know. Maybe it's stupid..."

It was an amazing drawing, but the reference was lost on me. "I remind you of an elephant?"

"Yes. An elephant never forgets. You want something that symbolizes how you got to this point in your life, well, there it is. You said you'd never forget what your family did to you, and you shouldn't either. You should remember it always. Because you should also never forget how strong it made you. And elephants are the strongest animal, and they're larger than life, but they're also incredibly gentle and peaceful. And that's what you are."

Oh.

He added, "And the leaves, well, they signify a change in season, passing of time and of course new growth. I thought they were fitting."

I couldn't believe how much meaning he put into one drawing. I looked closer at the drawing, at the faint circles in the blue ink. They weren't circles. "Are those music notes?"

Andrew nodded. "It's the first bar of 'Hallelujah.'"

My heart squeezed, tripped, and fell in my chest, and tears sprang to my eyes. "Oh."

He looked alarmed. "If you don't like it—"

"Like it? It's perfect. It couldn't be more perfect. No one has ever... no one..." I couldn't speak, and a stupid tear rolled down my cheek. I scrubbed my face with the back of my hand.

Andrew looked horrified. "You weren't supposed to cry."

I snorted back more tears. "No, it's just that it's perfect. Completely perfect." I handed the drawing around for the others to see it. I kissed Andrew, not caring that our friends were watching. "Did you have any colours in mind?"

Andrew made a face. "It was the colours that I couldn't decide. You see, colour and shading is paramount in what I do when I draw at work, but for you, I just couldn't decide. I wanted primary colours: red, blue, green. Because from those, all colours are made. And that's what I think of when I think of you. The basis of all colours and light..." His words finished in a mumble.

The basis of all colours and light.

My voice was thick and filled with unshed tears. "Oh."

Andrew shrugged. "But primary colours won't look so great in a tattoo."

"Emilio will make it work," I said, finally finding my voice.

I looked at Emilio, but he was studying Andrew's pen-drawn elephant. "Yes, of course," he said, not looking up from the piece of paper. "This is really good," Emilio said. "Like, *really* good. You've adapted it for a tattoo like a pro."

"Oh," Andrew said, blushing. "It's just a rough draft. I'll redo it properly if Spencer says it's what he wants."

"I want that one," I said adamantly, pointing at the piece of paper. "Done in red, blue, and green."

"But it's just a drawing I did on the plane." Andrew was looking at me like I'd lost my mind. "While you were asleep, I just watched you, and I know that sounds creepy, but all I could think was how you can see the real person when they're peaceful, and that probably sounds really stupid."

"That," I replied softly, "is why I want that drawing."

"But it's not perfect."

I smiled at him. "It's perfect for me."

EPILOGUE

TWO YEARS LATER

I hung up the phone and smiled at Helen. "Grand opening in eight weeks."

Andrew's mother was leaning against my office desk, her hands to her mouth. "Oh, I'm so proud of you."

"It was mostly Lewis's doing." I deflected her compliment. But the Archer Cohen Foundation in Sydney was just two months away from opening its doors. In the two years since Andrew and I got back from Sydney, I'd been in constant contact with Lewis and giving him the idea of this project set alight a spark in him. He'd taken the loss of our brother very hard, and building a foundation, a shelter and safe place for LGBTIQ people, was his way of grieving. Because he couldn't help Archie when he'd needed it, he was now helping others. A tangible reflection of his guilt maybe, but a positive one.

I'd helped him as much as I could, as did Helen. She freely offered her business model to him, and anytime he had questions, needed help, he came to us. Our father wasn't too happy about the venture, to say the least. But Lewis looked him right in the eye and said if he didn't like it, he'd lose his last and only child. My father knew nothing of my input, but Lewis told me I had to be there on opening night, and there was no way I would let him down. "Let him see us," Lewis had said. "He has no ties to this foundation, at all." Lewis had been very certain to keep it that way. "It's our money, our fundraising. He can't touch it. And when he sees you standing with me on opening night, I hope it eats him alive."

I'd tried to reason that his position at Atoll Hotels would be in jeopardy, but Lewis wouldn't be swayed. "There are more important things, Spence. I know where my loyalties lie. Right where they should have been all along."

His words put a lump in my throat. "I'm proud of you," I'd told him, just moments before Andrew's mother said those very words to me.

"You and Andrew will have to go," Helen said. "Take a few weeks off, spend time with Lewis. Travel, relax. You've earned it."

I smiled at her. "Thanks. I'll check that Andrew can get the time off before I agree."

I'd started helping Helen at the Acacia Foundation, searching out at-risk teens and young adults, subject to abuse and discrimination because of their sexuality or gender. It was a liaison-officer-type role. These kids could relate to me, and I to them. In hindsight, it was the perfect role for me. What started as a case-only helping hand became an almost full-time job. My days as a relationship-fixer were long over. I now did four days a week at the Acacia Foundation and still helped Emilio at his shop a day or two a week as well. I'd moved into Andrew's place about a year ago, so me helping Emilio out was a good excuse to hang out with him. We still did our Sunday brunch at the shop every week without fail.

Maybe I could ask Yanni if he wanted to be a guest speaker at the opening night in Sydney. If anyone could vouch for the success of such foundations, it was him. Peter would undoubtedly go with him: they'd been inseparable since they first met. Their friendship became so much more than a love for silent films. It had been a long, two-year road for them, but a very far-removed Yanni from the one I first met, now called himself Peter's *well-kept twink*, bossing him around lavishly. Peter gave into every whim with only fondness in his eyes, yet it was clear to everyone just how much Yanni adored him. Yanni idolised him. They truly had the whole daddy-kink thing down to a fine art, and I claimed them to be my greatest relationship success story... besides mine and Andrew's, of course.

"Oh, here's Andrew now," Helen said, breaking me from my reverie.

And wasn't he a sight for sore eyes. Man, I could just drink him in. Two years on and seeing him still tripped my heart over.

Helen chuckled. "You know what my favourite thing is about you, Spencer?"

I looked from where Andrew was walking in and stared at her. God, this could go either way. "Um, no?"

"The look on your face when you see my son. I mean, I'm so very pleased that he's happy and how well you treat him, of course. But when he walks in here and you lay eyes on him, your whole face changes. It's like a light switches on from the inside."

"Oh."

"He takes your breath away."

I cleared my throat. "He does."

Helen sighed serenely just as Andrew stuck his head around the open doorframe. "Can I come in?"

"Of course," his mother said with a loving smile. She stood gracefully and breezed to the door. "I was just telling Spencer it was adorable how he looked at you."

Andrew pressed his lips together and looked at me apologetically.

I shrugged and shook my head. "I'm not embarrassed."

Helen kissed Andrew's cheek and disappeared down the hall. Andrew walked in, and leaning down, he kissed me.

I breathed in his scent. In two years, my love for how he smelled hadn't lessened at all. "To what do I owe this pleasure?"

He leaned his arse against my desk. "Can't I drop by and see my boyfriend at work?"

"You can."

"I had to run some errands for the boss's boss and was just a block or two over. I can't stay, though. I'm expected back before close of business. Just wanted to check you're still on for tonight?"

Andrew had lined up drinks with everyone at The Bassline, a relatively new jazz bar that he loved. It wasn't too unusual; he'd organised a few drinks sessions there for all our friends before. The crowd was always good, the food was great, and the music was awesome. "Wouldn't want to be anywhere else."

"Want me to pick you up?"

I checked my watch. It was a little after four already. "I'll have to meet you there. Is that okay? I have a few hours of work left to do yet, and it'll be quicker if I just go straight there." I looked down at what I was wearing. It was black trousers, a grey button down shirt, and black suspenders. "Is this okay?"

"You always look great."

I waited while he looked me up and down. He loved it when I wore suspenders, though he'd not said as much, his eyes gave him away. I put my thumb under the elastic and pulled on it. "I can do a private showing if you'd like?"

He kinda laughed me off, blushing a little. I'd expected him to admonish me, but instead he said, "Later."

I groaned out a laugh. "You're killing me. How am I supposed to work thinking about that?"

He grinned. "Yes, on that note, I should get going before... well, before we get you into trouble at work." He stood to leave. "I'll see you tonight."

"Oh, before I forget. I just spoke to Lewis. He asked if we could be there for the grand opening in eight weeks."

His reply was immediate and straight from the heart. "Wouldn't miss it."

"Your mum suggested we have a bit of a vacation while we're there?" I shrugged. "Check with work and see if you can."

"I will." He leaned down and kissed me again. "And about tonight, don't be too late." And he walked out with a smile.

***

BY THE TIME I walked into the bar, I was about half an hour later than I'd said I would be. There was quite a crowd, and I had to push my way through to the back where I knew Andrew would be. Closest to the stage and the swinging jazz music, as usual.

Except he wasn't. He was at the end of the bar with Emilio, and I watched with shocked amusement as they both threw back shots. Alright then. That was unusual. Emilio clapped his hand on Andrew's arm, just as Andrew spotted me. He said something, which I couldn't hear, but Emilio turned around and grinned when he saw me. "Hey, Spencer!" he cried. "Lemme get you a drink."

He ordered another round of tequila, which told me something was up. Emilio rarely drank liquor, and the last time he had tequila was the day my visa for permanent residence came through. He swore after that night he'd never drink it again, so something was definitely up.

"What's the occasion?" I asked, then downed the shot.

Andrew almost swallowed his shot glass, so Emilio answered. "It's Friday."

Jesus. The alcohol burned from my scalp to my toes. I exhaled through it and fixed my gaze on Andrew. He let out a laugh and seemed out of sorts. "Everything okay?"

He licked his lips and nodded quickly. "Everything's fine. Except that tequila is really not good."

I leaned in to talk over the music. "So why are you having it?"

Andrew answered with a nervous laugh. "Oh, it was Emilio's idea."

Okay then. Something was *most definitely* up.

That was when I looked over at the tables. Everyone was there. I mean, everyone. His friends, my friends, his parents? *What the fuck?*

Then the band stopped, and before I could ask Andrew what was going on, the barman said, "Hey buddy, what can I get for ya?"

I turned to him. "Bottled water? Times two." I figured if Andrew had had some shots of tequila, he could probably use some water. I put a twenty on the bar just as the band singer spoke over the microphone.

"Ladies and Gentlemen," she said. "We'll be taking a short break, but before we do, we have a special guest."

Almost everyone in the bar was now facing the stage, so I did too. Only to see Andrew walking over to the lady with the microphone.

Okay, things were officially fucking weird.

The stage lights made it hard to tell if he was pale green from stage fright or bright red from embarrassment. He looked a bit of both. Then he sat at the piano.

My drinks and change forgotten, I stared at him. What the hell was he doing? He hated playing in front of crowds. Hated it. He'd once likened it to being set on fire. He adjusted the microphone, and I could see his hands were shaking. "Um, I have," he said too loudly, then backed off a bit to start again. He cleared his throat. "I have something," but then he looked down and mumbled something no one could hear. The microphone made a high-pitched keening sound, and a few people somewhere in the crowd laughed.

Andrew put his hands to the keys. "Um."

Someone in the crowd called out, "Can you play? Or you just gonna stutter into the microphone?"

Before I could tell that arsehole to shut the fuck up, Andrew zipped through the first few bars of "The Flight of the Bumblebee", his fingers skimming over the ivories with well-practiced finesse, which was pianist code for "Hey arsehole, shut the fuck up."

The audience clapped and laughed, and Andrew ran his hands through his hair. "Um, Spencer?"

I hadn't realised I'd taken a few steps toward the stage. I seemed to be the only one on the dance floor; the entire bar was staring at us.

Andrew took a deep breath to centre himself and put his hands back to the keys, and he started to play. In our two years together, Andrew had never played me this.

"Hallelujah."

I didn't even know Andrew knew how to play this song... And then he started to sing.

And sweet mother of God, deep, nervous, and perfect, Andrew had the voice of an angel. So different from Jeff Buckley, so sweet and raspy and reverent. He sang about sacred chords, and baffled kings, and beauty in the moonlight.

I couldn't fathom how difficult it must have been for him to do this. Yet, there he was. Doing it for me. My stupid heart was thumping erratically, and my stupid brain couldn't process what I was seeing.

I looked behind me to see Lola and Emilio, Gabe and Daniela, everyone smiling at me like they knew what was going on. They knew he was going to play the piano and sing for me?

I turned back just as the other musicians were taking the stage. The drummer joined in, then the bass, the trumpet, and the woman sung along with Andrew about marble arches and victory marches, and the whole band played the song like they wrote it.

The crescendo was phenomenal and I could feel the beat resonating in my chest. But before the final bridge, the song morphed into something else. It was a medley of songs that the audience cheered for until the music evened out into just one song.

I wasn't *as* familiar with this song, though I knew what it was. The woman sang soulfully, beautifully, about it being a beautiful night, that love was such a wonderful thing.

Andrew stood up from the piano and stepped off the stage. He looked right at me and the music cut. Complete silence filled the room, then our group of friends and family, led by Emilio and Lola and Andrew's parents, sang the next line.

"If I could, I totally would, marry you."

I spun to look at them and then turned back to Andrew to find him on bended knee in front of me.

I have no clue if the band still played. I don't know if our friends still sang. I don't know what the audience behind me did...

All there was, all I could see was Andrew.

He took a silver ring from his pocket and held it on the palm of his hand. He whispered, or maybe he shouted over the noise my brain shut out. I still couldn't tell. But I heard him just fine.

"Spencer Cohen, if there was a magazine called *The Only Man I Want to Spend My Life With*, you'd be on the cover, of every edition, ever. You are everything to me. You deserve more love and happiness than I can give you in one lifetime, but I'd sure like to try. Marry me. Please."

I tried to speak. I tried not to cry. I failed miserably at both. *He wanted to marry me?* All I could do was nod.

Andrew stood and threw his arms around me. He buried his face in my neck, and we were quickly surrounded by a sea of hugging people. We were pulled apart and hugged and congratulated individually, which was nice and all, but they were not the arms I wanted to be in. I unpeeled Lola from around me and found Andrew being embraced by his father. I tapped Allan on the shoulder, cutting in on this dance of hugs, and waited for him to step aside.

Andrew stared at me and let out a nervous breath. My voice was thick with unshed tears. "You played 'Hallelujah.'"

"I *sang* it. Which was quite possibly the worst thing I've ever done. I broke my leg when I was eight. That was reasonably unpleasant, but singing wins. I thought playing the piano would be bad enough, but singing? I can't believe... I don't even know what I was thinking when I planned this."

It certainly explained the shots of tequila. I laughed and pulled him in for a soul-soothing hug. Having Andrew pressed against me was a medicinal thing. He mended me in ways he could never understand. "You were thinking it would be the most perfect proposal ever. And you put Jeff Buckley to shame."

He smiled into my neck. "You liked it?"

"Loved it." I pulled back and held his face in my hands and softly pressed my lips to his. My head was still spinning. "I can't believe you did that. Do you really want to marry me?"

"There is nothing in this world I want more," he whispered, "than to call you my husband."

His sincerity, his honesty, and overwhelming love brought tears to my eyes. "I love you Andrew, and if there was a magazine called *The Only Man I Want to Spend My Life With*, I wouldn't be on *every* cover. You'd be on the limited edition one. You know, just for me."

He smiled so beautifully. "I was going to get a magazine made up with you on the cover called *Who I Want To Marry*, but thought you might think it silly."

I burst out laughing. "It would have been great. But you and what you did here"—I waved at the stage and at our friends—"was so perfect."

"Maybe we could do magazine covers for our wedding invitations," he said. I wasn't sure if he was joking or not, but his mother squealed beside us.

"Oh, that is a fabulous idea!"

And so it began. Helen, Sarah, and Lola were already planning our entire wedding and the rest of our lives, by the sound of it. I didn't care. Because in that moment, the background music started to play. Etta James began to sing "At Last" and I slow, slow danced with Andrew in the middle of our friends and family. I buried my face into Andrew's neck and he held me even tighter.

Etta James' soulful voice filled my chest with words of loneliness being over, and how life was now a song. She sang about finding dreams and heaven. And she was right, because I held him in my arms.

At last. At last, indeed.

The End

SUICIDE HELPLINES

If you, or someone you know, needs help. Just remember, you're not alone...

http://www.suicide.org/international-suicide-hotlines.html
http://www.iasp.info/resources/Crisis_Centres
http://www.befrienders.org/need-to-talk
http://www.thetrevorproject.org/

For a Cyber community for gay and lesbian teenagers all over the world, go to:
Youth Guard Services

Or

Here are the direct suicide helplines, worldwide.
(credit to http://im-just-lucy.tumblr.com/suicidehotlines)

Albania: 127
    Argentina: (54-11) 4758-2554
    Australia: 13 11 14
    Austria: 142

Barbados: (246) 4299999

Belgium: 106

Botswana: 3911270

Brazil: +55 51 211 2888

Canada - Greater Vancouver: 604-872-3311

Canada - Toll free-Howe Sound/Sunshine Coast: 18666613311

Canada - TTY: 1-866-872-0113

Canada - BC-wide: 1-800-SUICIDE (784-2433)

China: 0800-810-1117

China (Mobile/IP/extension users): 010-8295-1332

Croatia: (01) 4833-888

Cyprus: +357 77 77 72 67

Denmark: +45 70 201 201

Estonia (1): 126

Estonia (2): 127

Estonia (3): 646 6666

Fiji (1): 679 670565

Fiji (2): 679 674364

Finland: 01019-0071

France: (+33) (0)9 51 11 61 30

Germany (1): 0800 1110 111

Germany (2): 0800 1110 222

Germany (youth): 0800 1110 333

Ghana: 233 244 846 701

Greece: (0) 30 210 34 17 164

Hungary: (46) 323 888

India: 2549 7777

Ireland (1): +44 (0) 8457 90 90 90

Ireland (2): +44 (0) 8457 90 91 92

Ireland (3): 1850 60 90 90

Ireland (4): 1850 60 90 91

Israel: 1201

Italy: 199 284 284

Japan (1): 03 5774 0992

Japan (2): 03 3498 0231

Kenya: +254 20 3000378/2051323

Liberia: 06534308

Lithuania: 8-800 2 8888

Malaysia (1): (063) 92850039

Malaysia (2): (063) 92850279

Malaysia (3): (063) 92850049

Malta: 179

Mauritius: (230) 800 93 93

Namibia: (09264) 61-232-221

Netherlands: 0900-0767

New Zealand (1): (09) 522 2999

New Zealand (2): 0800 111 777

Norway: +47 815 33 300

Papua New Guinea: 675 326 0011

Philippines: 02 -896 - 9191

Poland (1): +48 527 00 00

Poland (2): +48 89 92 88

Portugal: (808) 200 204

Samoa: 32000

Serbia: 32000

Singapore: 1800- 221 4444

South Africa: 0861 322 322

Sweden (1): 020 22 00 60

Sweden (2): 020 22 00 70

Switzerland: 143

Thailand: (02) 713-6793

Ukraine: 058

United Kingdom (1): 08457 909090

United Kingdom (2): +44 1603 611311

United Kingdom (3): +44 (0) 8457 90 91 92

United Kingdom (4): 1850 60 90 90
United Kingdom (5): 1850 60 90 91
United States of America: 1-800-273-TALK (8255)
Zimbabwe (1): (263) 09 65000
Zimbabwe (2): 0800 9102

ABOUT THE AUTHOR

N.R. Walker is an Australian author, who loves her genre of gay romance. She loves writing and spends far too much time doing it, but wouldn't have it any other way.

She is many things: a mother, a wife, a sister, a writer. She has pretty, pretty boys who live in her head, who don't let her sleep at night unless she gives them life with words.

She likes it when they do dirty, dirty things... but likes it even more when they fall in love.

She used to think having people in her head talking to her was weird, until one day she happened across other writers who told her it was normal.

She's been writing ever since...

Exchange of Hearts

The Spencer Cohen Series, Book One

The Spencer Cohen Series, Book Two

The Spencer Cohen Series, Book Three

The Spencer Cohen Series, Yanni's Story

Blood & Milk

The Weight Of It All

A Very Henry Christmas (The Weight of It All 1.5)

Perfect Catch

Switched

Imago

Imagines

Imagoes

Red Dirt Heart Imago

On Davis Row

Finders Keepers

Evolved

Galaxies and Oceans

Private Charter

Nova Praetorian

A Soldier's Wish

Upside Down

The Hate You Drink

Sir

Tallowwood

Reindeer Games

The Dichotomy of Angels

Throwing Hearts

Pieces of You - Missing Pieces #1

Pieces of Me - Missing Pieces #2

Pieces of Us - Missing Pieces #3

Lacuna

Tic-Tac-Mistletoe

Bossy

Code Red

Dearest Milton James

Dearest Malachi Keogh

Christmas Wish List

Code Blue

Davo

The Kite

Learning Curve

Merry Christmas Cupid

To the Moon and Back

TITLES IN AUDIO:

Cronin's Key

Cronin's Key II

Cronin's Key III

Red Dirt Heart

Red Dirt Heart 2

Red Dirt Heart 3

Red Dirt Heart 4

The Weight Of It All

Switched

Point of No Return

Breaking Point

Starting Point

Spencer Cohen Book One

Spencer Cohen Book Two

Spencer Cohen Book Three

Yanni's Story

On Davis Row

Evolved

Elements of Retrofit

Clarity of Lines

Sense of Place

Blind Faith

Through These Eyes

Blindside

Finders Keepers

Galaxies and Oceans

Nova Praetorian

Upside Down

Sir

Tallowwood

Imago

Throwing Hearts

Sixty Five Hours

Taxes and TARDIS

The Dichotomy of Angels

The Hate You Drink

Pieces of You

Pieces of Me

Pieces of Us

Tic-Tac-Mistletoe

Lacuna

Bossy

Code Red

Learning to Feel

Dearest Milton James

Dearest Malachi Keogh

Three's Company

Christmas Wish List

Code Blue

Davo

The Kite

Learning Curve

Merry Christmas Cupid

SERIES COLLECTIONS:

Red Dirt Heart Series

Turning Point Series

Thomas Elkin Series

Spencer Cohen Series

Imago Series

Blind Faith Series

FREE READS:

Sixty Five Hours

Learning to Feel

His Grandfather's Watch (And The Story of Billy and Hale)

The Twelfth of Never (Blind Faith 3.5)

Twelve Days of Christmas (Sixty Five Hours Christmas)

Best of Both Worlds

TRANSLATED TITLES:

ITALIAN

Fiducia Cieca (Blind Faith)

Attraverso Questi Occhi (Through These Eyes)

Preso alla Sprovvista (Blindside)

Il giorno del Mai (Blind Faith 3.5)

Cuore di Terra Rossa Serie (Red Dirt Heart Series)

Natale di terra rossa (Red dirt Christmas)

Intervento di Retrofit (Elements of Retrofit)

A Chiare Linee (Clarity of Lines)

Senso D'appartenenza (Sense of Place)

Spencer Cohen Serie (including Yanni's Story)

Punto di non Ritorno (Point of No Return)

Punto di Rottura (Breaking Point)

Punto di Partenza (Starting Point)

Imago (Imago)

Il desiderio di un soldato (A Soldier's Wish)

Scambiato (Switched)

Galassie e Oceani (Galaxies and Oceans)

FRENCH

Confiance Aveugle (Blind Faith)

A travers ces yeux: Confiance Aveugle 2 (Through These Eyes)

Aveugle: Confiance Aveugle 3 (Blindside)

À Jamais (Blind Faith 3.5)

Cronin's Key Series

Au Coeur de Sutton Station (Red Dirt Heart)

Partir ou rester (Red Dirt Heart 2)

Faire Face (Red Dirt Heart 3)

Trouver sa Place (Red Dirt Heart 4)

Le Poids de Sentiments (The Weight of It All)

Un Noël à la sauce Henry (A Very Henry Christmas)

Une vie à Refaire (Switched)

Evolution (Evolved)

Galaxies & Océans

Qui Trouve, Garde (Finders Keepers)

Sens Dessus Dessous (Upside Down)

Spencer Cohen Series

GERMAN

Flammende Erde (Red Dirt Heart)

Lodernde Erde (Red Dirt Heart 2)

Sengende Erde (Red Dirt Heart 3)

Ungezähmte Erde (Red Dirt Heart 4)

Vier Pfoten und ein bisschen Zufall (Finders Keepers)

Ein Kleines bisschen Versuchung (The Weight of It All)

Ein Kleines Bisschen Fur Immer (A Very Henry Christmas)

Weil Leibe uns immer Bliebt (Switched)

Drei Herzen eine Leibe (Three's Company)

Über uns die Sterne, zwischen uns die Liebe (Galaxies and Oceans)

Unnahbares Herz (Blind Faith 1)

Sehendes Herz (Blind Faith 2)

Hoffnungsvolles Herz (Blind Faith 3)

Verträumtes Herz (Blind Faith 3.5)

Thomas Elkin: Verlangen in neuem Design

Traummann töpfern leicht gemacht (Throwing Hearts)

THAI

Sixty Five Hours (Thai translation)

Finders Keepers (Thai translation)

SPANISH

Sesenta y Cinco Horas (Sixty Five Hours)

Los Doce Días de Navidad

Código Rojo (Code Red)

Código Azul (Code Blue)

Queridísimo Milton James

Queridísimo Malachi Keogh

El Peso de Todo (The Weight of it All)

Tres Muérdagos en Raya: Serie Navidad en Hartbridge

Lista De Deseos Navideños: Serie Navidad en Hartbridge

Spencer Cohen Libro Uno

Spencer Cohen Libro Dos

Spencer Cohen Libro Tres

La Historia de Yanni

Davo

Feliz Navidad Cupido: Serie Navidad en Hartbridge

CHINESE

Blind Faith

www.ingramcontent.com/pod-product-compliance
Lightning Source LLC
Chambersburg PA
CBHW050530190726
48284CB00003B/1007